Armitage, Armitage, Fly Away Home

BOOKS BY JOAN AIKEN

For Young Readers

ARMITAGE, ARMITAGE, FLY AWAY HOME
NIGHTBIRDS ON NANTUCKET
BLACK HEARTS IN BATTERSEA
THE WOLVES OF WILLOUGHBY CHASE

For Adult Readers

THE CRYSTAL CROW
DARK INTERVAL
BEWARE OF THE BOUQUET
THE FORTUNE HUNTERS
THE SILENCE OF HERONDALE

Armitage, Armitage, Fly Away Home

by Joan Aiken

Illustrated by Betty Fraser

DOUBLEDAY & COMPANY, INC., GARDEN CITY, NEW YORK

Design by Jeanette Portelli

1692247

Contents

Armitage, Armitage, Fly Away Home

Prelude

Once upon a time two people met, fell in love, and got married. Their names were Mr. and Mrs. Armitage. While they were on their honeymoon, staying at a farm near the Sussex coast, they often spent whole days on the beach, which at that point was reached by a path over a high shingle ridge. The sea was beautifully empty, the weather was beautifully warm, and the beach was beautifully peaceful.

One hot, sleepy afternoon the Armitages had been bathing and were lying on the shingle afterwards, sunning themselves, when Mrs. Armitage said,

"Darling, are you awake?"

Her husband snored, and then said, "Eh? Whatsay, darling?"

"This business of living happily after," she said rather

thoughtfully, "it sounds all right but—well—what do we actually do with ourselves all the time?"

"Oh," Mr. Armitage said yawning. "'Spose I go to the office every day and you look after the house and cook dinner—that sort of thing?"

"I see. You don't think," she said doubtfully, "that sounds a little *dull?*"

"Dull? Certainly not." He went back to sleep again. But his wife turned restlessly onto her stomach and scooped with her fingers among the smooth, rattling brown and yellow and white and gray pebbles, which were all warm and smelled of salt.

Presently she exclaimed, "Oh!"

"Whassamarrer?" Mr. Armitage mumbled.

"I've found a stone with a hole." She held up her finger with the stone fitting neatly over it—a round white chalk-stone with a hole in the middle.

"'Markable," said her husband without opening his eyes.

"When I was little," Mrs. Armitage said, "I used to call those wishing-stones."

"Mmm."

She rolled onto her back again and admired the white stone fitting so snugly on her finger.

"I wish we'll live in a beautiful house in a beautiful village with a big garden and a field and at least one ghost," she said sleepily.

"That's Uncle Cuthbert's house," her husband said. "He's just left it to me. Meant to tell you."

"And I wish we'll have two children called Mark and Harriet with cheerful energetic natures who will never mope or sulk or get bored. And I hope lots of interesting and un-usual things will happen to them. It would be nice if they had a fairy godmother, for instance," she went on dreamily.

"Here, hold on!" muttered her husband.

"And a few magic wishes. And a phoenix or something out of the ordinary for a pet."

"Whoa, wait a minute! Be a bit distracting, wouldn't it, all those things going on? Never know what to expect next! And what would the neighbors think?"

"Bother the neighbors! Well," she allowed, "we could have a special day for interesting and unusual things to happen —say, Mondays. But not *always* Mondays, and not *only* Mondays, or that would get a bit dull too."

"You don't really believe in that stone, do you?" Mr. Armitage said anxiously.

"Only half."

"Well how about taking it off, now, and throwing it in the sea, before you wish for anything else?"

But the stone would not come off her finger.

When they had pushed and pulled and tugged until her finger was beginning to be a bit sore, Mrs. Armitage said, "We'd better go back to the farm. Mrs. Tulliver will get it off with soap, or butter. And you're getting as red as a lobster."

When they reached the top of the shingle ridge, Mrs. Armitage turned round and looked at the wide expanse of peaceful, silky, gray-blue sea.

"It's beautiful," she sighed, "very beautiful. But it would be nice to see something come out of it, once in a way. Like the sea-serpent."

No sooner had she spoken those words than a huge, green, gnarled, shining, horny head came poking up out of the sea. It was all covered with weeds and bumps and barnacles, like the bottom of some old, old ship. And it was followed by miles and miles and *miles* of body, and it stared at them with two pale, oysterish eyes and opened a mouth as large as Wookey Hole.

With great presence of mind Mrs. Armitage said, "Not today, thank you. Sorry you've been troubled. Down, sir! Heel. Go home, now, good serpent, I've got nothing for you."

With a sad, wailing hoot, like a ship's siren, the monster submerged again.

"For heaven's sake!" said Mr. Armitage. "The sooner we get that stone off your finger, the better it will be."

They walked on quite fast across the four fields between the beach and the farm. Every now and then Mrs. Armitage opened her mouth to speak, and whenever she did so, Mr. Armitage kindly but firmly clapped his hand over it to stop her.

Outside the farm they met four-year-old Vicky Tulliver, swinging on the gate and singing one of the songs she was always making up:

> "Two white ducks and
> Two white hens
> Two white turkeys
> Sitting on the fence—"

"Do you know where your Mummy is?" Mr. Armitage asked.

Vicky stopped singing long enough to say, "In the kitchen," so the Armitages went there and Mrs. Tulliver gave them a knob of beautiful fresh butter to loosen the stone. But it still wouldn't come off. So they tried soap and water, olive oil, tractor oil, clotted cream, and neat's foot oil. And still the stone would not come off.

"Deary me, what can we try next?" said Mrs. Tulliver. "Your poor finger's all red and swole."

"Oh, goodness, I wish it would come off," sighed Mrs. Armitage. And then, of course, she felt it loosen its hold at once. "Thank you, stone," she whispered. And just before she slipped it off, she breathed one last request: "Dear stone, please don't let me ever be bored with living happily ever after."

"Well!" said Mrs. Tulliver, looking at the stone. "Did you ever, then! Vicky, you've got the littlest fingers, 'spose you take and drop that stone in the well, afore it sticks on any other body the same way."

So Vicky took the white stone and hung it on her tiny forefinger, where it dangled loosely, and she went out to the well singing,

> "Two white heifers
> Two white goats
> Two white sheep an'
> Two white shoats
> Two white geese an'
> Two white ponies
> Two white puppies
> Two white coneys
> Two white ducks an'
> Two white hens
> Two white turkeys
> Sitting on the fence—
> Two white kittens
> Sitting in the sun
> I wish I had 'em
> Every one!"

And with that she tossed the white stone into the well.

"Deary me," said Mrs. Tulliver, looking out the kitchen window into the farmyard. "Snow in June, then?"

But of course it wasn't snow. It was all the white creatures Vicky had wished for, pecking and fluttering and frisking and flapping and mooing. Mr. Tulliver was quite astonished when he came home from haymaking, and as for Vicky, she thought it was her birthday and Easter and Christmas and August Bank Holiday all rolled into one.

But Mr. and Mrs. Armitage packed their cases and caught a train and went home to Uncle Cuthbert's house, where they settled down to begin living happily ever after.

And they were never, never bored. . . .

Yes, but Today Is Tuesday

Monday was the day on which unusual things were allowed, and even expected to happen at the Armitage house.

It was on a Monday, for instance, that two knights of the Round Table came and had a combat on the lawn, because they insisted that nowhere else was flat enough. And on another Monday two albatrosses nested on the roof, laid three eggs, knocked off most of the tiles, and then deserted the nest; Agnes, the cook, made the eggs into an omelet but it tasted too strongly of fish to be considered a success. And on another Monday, all the potatoes in a sack in the larder turned into the most beautiful Venetian glass apples, and Mrs. Epis, who came in two days a week to help with the cleaning, sold them to a rag-and-bone man for a shilling. So the Armitages were quite prepared for surprises on a Monday and, if by any chance the parents had gone out during the day, they were apt to open the front door rather cautiously on their return, in case a dromedary should charge at them, which had happened on a particularly notable Monday before Christmas. Then they would go very quietly and carefully into the sitting room, and sit down, and fortify themselves with sherry before Mark and Harriet came in and told them precisely *what* had happened since breakfast time.

You will see, therefore, that this story is all the more remarkable because it happened on a Tuesday.

It began at breakfast time, when Mark came into the dining room and announced that there was a unicorn in the garden.

"Nonsense," said his father. "Today is Tuesday."

"I can't help it," said Mark. "Just you go and look. It's standing out among the peonies, and it's a beauty, I can tell you."

Harriet started to her feet, but Mrs. Armitage was firm. "Finish your shredded wheat first, Harriet. After all, today *is* Tuesday."

So Harriet very unwillingly finished her shredded wheat and gulped down her coffee, and then she rushed into the garden. There, sure enough, knee-deep in the great clump of peonies at the end of the lawn stood a unicorn, looking about rather inquiringly. It was a most lovely creature—snow-white all over, with shining green eyes and a twisted mother-of-pearl horn in the middle of its forehead. Harriet noticed with interest that this horn and the creature's hoofs had a sort of greenish gleam to them, as if they were slightly transparent and lit up from within. The unicorn seemed quite pleased to see Harriet, and she rubbed its velvety nose for a minute or two. Then it turned away and took a large mouthful of peony blossoms. But almost at once it spat them out again and looked at her reproachfully with its lustrous green eyes.

Harriet reflected. Then she saw Mark coming out, and went towards him. "I think it's hungry," she remarked. "What do you suppose unicorns like to eat?"

"Do you think perhaps honeycomb?" Mark suggested. So they went secretly to the larder by the back door and took a large honeycomb out on a platter. Mark held it to the unicorn, first rolling up his sleeves so that the creature should not dribble honey onto him. It sniffed the honey in a cautious manner, and finally crunched it up in two mouthfuls and looked pleased.

"Now, do you suppose," said Harriet, "that it would like a drink of milk?" And she fetched it some milk in a blue bowl. The unicorn lapped it up gratefully.

"I think it must have been traveling all night, don't you?" said Mark. "Look it's got burrs all tangled up in its tail. I'll comb them out."

At this moment their father came out into the garden for his after-breakfast stroll. At the sight of the unicorn he paused, stared at it, and finally remarked:

"Nonsense. Today is *Tuesday*. It must have got left over from last night. It was very careless of you not to have noticed it, Harriet." The unicorn looked at him amiably and began to wash itself like a cat. Mark went off to hunt for a large comb.

"Do you think we could ride it?" Harriet asked her father.

"Not at the moment," he answered, as the unicorn achieved a particularly graceful twist, and began licking the middle of its back. "If you ask me, I should think it would be like riding the sea-serpent. But, of course, you're welcome to try, when it has finished washing."

Mrs. Epis came out into the garden.

"There's a policeman at the door," she said, "and Mrs. Armitage says will you come and deal with him, sir, please."

"A policeman," Harriet observed to herself. "They don't usually come on a Tuesday." She followed her father to the front door.

This policeman was different from the usual one. Harriet could not remember ever seeing him before. He looked at a piece of paper in his hand and said,

"I have an inquiry to make about a unicorn. Is it true that you are keeping one without a license?"

"I don't know about keeping it," said Mr. Armitage. "There's certainly one in the garden, but it's only just arrived. We hadn't really decided to keep it yet. I must say, you're very prompt about looking us up."

"Please let's pay the license and keep it," whispered Harriet very urgently.

"Well, how much is this precious license, before we go any further?" asked Mr. Armitage.

The policeman consulted his piece of paper again. "Ten thousand gold pieces," he read out.

"But that's absurd. Today is Tuesday!" exclaimed Mr. Armitage. "Besides we haven't got that in the house. As a matter of fact I doubt if we've got so much as one gold piece in the house."

Harriet did not wait to hear what happened after that. She went out to the unicorn with two large tears in her eyes.

"Why do you have to have such an enormous license?" she asked it. "You might have known we couldn't keep you."

A large green drop of water the size of a plum dropped down on her hand. It was the unicorn's tear.

Mark came across the lawn with a comb. Harriet felt too sad to tell him that they couldn't afford the unicorn. She watched him begin slowly and carefully combing the long tail. The unicorn looked round to see what was happening, and then gave an approving grunt and stood very upright and still.

"Good heavens!" said Mark. "Look what's fallen out of its tail. A gold piece! And here's another!" At every sweep of the comb, gold pieces tumbled out onto the grass, and soon there was a considerable pile of them.

"They'll do for the license!" exclaimed Harriet. "Quick, Mark, go on combing. We want ten thousand of them. Here are Father and the policeman coming to inspect it." She began feverishly counting the coins and sorting them into heaps of ten.

"It's going to take a terrible time," she remarked. "We might as well ask the policeman to check them."

The two men seemed rather astonished to see what was going on. Harriet had a feeling that the policeman was not altogether pleased. However, he knelt down and began helping to count out the coins. Just as Agnes came out to tell the children that their eleven o'clock bread-and-dripping was on the kitchen table, they finished the counting. The policeman gave Mr. Armitage a receipt and took himself off with the money in a bag over his shoulder. And Mr. Armitage looked at his watch and exclaimed that it was high time he did some work, and went indoors.

Mark and Harriet sat on the lawn, munching their bread-and-dripping and looking at the unicorn, which was smelling a rose with evident satisfaction.

"I wonder if it ought to be shod?" murmured Mark, looking at its greenish hoofs. "If we're going to ride it, I mean." They went over and examined the hoofs at close quarters. They looked rather worn and sore.

"I don't suppose it's used to stones and hard roads like ours," said Harriet. "You can see it's a foreign animal by the surprised look it has on its face all the time."

Mark agreed. "Would you like to be shod?" he asked the creature. It nodded intelligently. "Well, if that isn't good enough, I don't know what is." They made a halter out of a green dressing-gown cord of Harriet's, and led the unicorn down to the forge, where Mr. Ellis, the blacksmith, was leaning against a wall in the sun, reading the paper.

"Please, will you shoe our unicorn for us?" asked Harriet.

"What, you two again!" exclaimed Mr. Ellis. "I thought today was Tuesday. First it's dromedaries, then unicorns. Thank 'eavens they've got 'oofs of a normal shape. Well, you lead 'im in, Master Mark. I'm not pining to have that there spike of his sticking into me breakfast."

The unicorn was beautifully shod, with light, small silvery shoes, and seemed very pleased with them.

"How much will that be?" Harriet asked.

"I'll have to look up in my list, if you'll excuse me," said Mr. Ellis. "I can't remember what it is offhand, for a unicorn. Cor', you won't 'alf have a time at the Toll Bridge at Potter's End, if you ever takes 'im that way." He went into the back of the forge, where the great bellows were, and found a grubby list. "Quagga, reindeer—no—farther on we want," and he ran his finger down to the end and started up. "Zebra, yak, wildebeest, waterbuck, unicorn. Twelve pieces of gold, please, Miss Harriet." Fortunately Mark had put the comb in his pocket, so there was no difficulty about combing twelve pieces out of the unicorn's tail. Then they started back home, fairly slowly, giving him time to get accustomed to the feel of his new shoes. He lifted his feet gingerly at first, as if they felt heavy, but soon he seemed to be used to them.

Back on the lawn he became quite lively, and pranced about, kicking up his heels.

"We haven't thought of a name for him," said Harriet. "What about Candleberry?"

"Why not?" said Mark, ". . . and *now* I am going to ride him."

The unicorn took very kindly to having riders on his back, except for an absent-minded habit of tossing his head, which on one occasion nearly impaled Harriet on his horn. They noticed that when he galloped he could remain off the ground for quite long stretches at a time.

"He can very nearly fly," said Harriet.

"Perhaps the air where he comes from is thicker," suggested Mark ingeniously. "Like the difference between salt and fresh water, you know."

And then, just as they were deciding to rig up a jump and see how high he would go, they saw a little old man in a red cloak standing on the lawn, watching them. Candleberry stood stock still and shivered all over, as if his skin had suddenly gone goosy.

"Good morning," said Harriet politely. "Do you want to speak to Mr. Armitage?"

But the little man had his eyes fixed on Candleberry. "How dare you steal one of my unicorns?" he said fiercely.

"I like that!" exclaimed Mark. "It came of its own accord. We never stole it."

"You will return it at once, or it will be the worse for you."

"After we've paid for its license too," chimed in Harriet.

"I never heard such cheek. We shouldn't dream of returning it. Obviously it ran away from you because it was unhappy. You can't have treated it properly."

"What!" the old man almost shrieked. "You accuse *me* of not knowing how to treat a unicorn!" He seemed nearly bursting with rage. "If you won't give it back, I'll make you. I'll cast a spell over it."

"Hold on," said Harriet. "We've had it shod. You haven't any power over it any more." Even she knew that.

At these words a terrible look crossed over the old man's face.

"You'll discover what it is to interfere with me," he said ominously, and struck his staff on the ground. Mark and Harriet with one accord grabbed hold of Candleberry's bridle. The whole place became pitch dark, and thunder rolled dreadfully overhead. A great wind whistled through the trees. Candleberry stamped and shivered. Then the gale caught up all three of them, and they were whisked away through the air. "Hang onto the bridle," shrieked Mark in Harriet's ear. "I can see the sea coming," she shrieked back. Indeed, down below them, and coming nearer every minute, was a raging sea with black waves as big as houses.

When the storm burst, Mr. and Mrs. Armitage were inside the house.

"I hope the children have the sense to shelter somewhere," said Mrs. Armitage. Her husband looked out at the weather and gave a yelp of dismay.

"All my young peas and beans! They'll be blown as flat as pancakes," he cried in agony, and rushed out into the garden. But as he went out, the wind dropped and the sun shone again. Mr. Armitage walked over the lawn, his eyes starting

in horror from his head. For all about the garden were one hundred unicorns!

He went back into the house in a state of collapse and told his wife. "My garden will be trampled to pieces," he moaned. "How will we ever get rid of them?"

"Perhaps Mark and Harriet will have some ideas," suggested Mrs. Armitage. But Mark and Harriet were nowhere to be found. Mrs. Epis was having hysterics in the kitchen. "It's not decent," was all she could say. She had come upon the unicorns unexpectedly, as she was hanging some tea-cloths on the line.

Agnes, oddly enough, was the one who had a practical idea.

"If you please, sir," she said. "I think my dad wouldn't mind three or four of those to use as plough horses. Someone told me that once you've got them trained, they're very cheap to feed."

So her father, Mr. Monks, came along, looked over the herd, and picked out five likely ones as farm horses. "And thank you kindly," he said.

"You don't know anyone else who'd be glad of a few, do you?" asked Mr. Armitage hopefully. "As you can see, we've got rather more than we know what to do with."

"I wouldn't be surprised but what old Farmer Meads could take some in. I'll ask him," Mr. Monks volunteered. "And there's old Gilbert the carter, and I believe as how someone said the milkman was looking for a new pony."

"Do ask them all," said Mr. Armitage desperately. "And look—stick this up on the village notice-board as you go past." He hastily scribbled a notice which he handed to Mr. Monks:

Unicorns given away. Quiet to ride or drive.

The rest of that day the Armitages were fully occupied in giving away unicorns to all applicants. "It's worse than trying to get rid of a family of kittens," said Mrs. Armitage. "And if they don't turn out well, we shall have to move away from the village. Oh, there's the artist who lives up on Pennington Hill. I'm sure he'd like a unicorn to carry his paints about for him."

All day there was no sign of Mark or Harriet, and the parents began to worry. "If it were Monday, now, it would be all right," they said, "but where can they be?"

Late in the evening, after they had disposed of the last unicorn to the baker's boy, and he had gone rejoicing along to Mr. Ellis (who was nearly at his wits' end by this time) to have it shod, Mark and Harriet trailed in, looking exhausted but content.

"Where *have* you been? And what *have* you done to your clothes?" Mrs. Armitage asked them.

"It wasn't our fault," Harriet said drowsily. "We were bewitched. We were blown over the sea, and we fell in. We would have been drowned, only a submarine rose up under us and took us into Brighton."

"And why didn't you come home straight off, pray?"

"Well, we had to earn some money for our bus fares. They won't take unicorn-gold in Brighton, I don't know why. So we organized a show with Candleberry on the beach and earned an awful lot. And then we had a huge tea, and Mark caught the bus, and I followed along by the side on Candleberry. He's terribly fast. He's asleep in the greenhouse now. We thought that would be a good place for him. What's the matter with the garden? It looks trampled."

Harriet's voice was trailing away with sleep.

"You two," said Mrs. Armitage, "are going straight to bed."

"But we *always* stay up to supper on Mondays," complained Mark in the middle of a vast yawn.

"Yes," said his father, "but today, as it happens, is Tuesday."

The Frozen Cuckoo

There was a good deal of trouble at breakfast. To begin with, Mr. Armitage was late, and that made Mrs. Armitage cross, as she always liked to have the meal over quickly on Mondays, so that the dining room could be turned out. Then she began reading her letters, and suddenly inquired:

"What is the date today?"

"The second," said Harriet.

"I thought so. Then that means she is coming today. How very inconsiderate."

"Who is coming today?"

"Your cousin Sarah."

"Oh no!" said Mark and Harriet together, in deep dismay. It is dreadful to have to say it of anybody, but their cousin Sarah was really a horrible girl. The only thing she seemed to enjoy was playing practical jokes, which she did the whole time. Nobody minds an occasional joke, but an endless course of sand in the brown-sugar bowl, grease on the stairs, and plastic spiders on the pillowcases soon become tiresome.

"It'll be apple-pie beds, apple-pie beds all the way," said Mark gloomily. "Can't you put her off?"

"No, Aunt Rachel has to go into hospital for an operation, so I'm afraid you'll just have to bear with her. She's coming at lunchtime."

Here Mr. Armitage arrived, and sat down rubbing his hands and saying: "The Christmas roses will be out any minute now."

"You bacon's cold," said his wife crossly. "Here are your letters."

He opened a long, important-looking one which had a lot of printed headings on it, and instantly began to puff and blow with rage.

"Evicted? Requisitioned? What's this? Notice to quit forthwith before 11 A.M., December the second. Who the dickens is this from?"

"Good gracious, my dear," said his wife, "what have you got there?"

"It's from the Board of Incantation," he replied, throwing the letter to her. "They've requisitioned this house, if you please, to make a seminary for young magicians, and we have notice to quit immediately."

"A. Whizzard," murmured Mrs. Armitage, looking at the signature. "Wasn't that the name of the man whose book you were so rude about in your review?"

"Yes, of course. I knew the name seemed familiar. A shockingly bad book on spells and runes."

"Oh dear," sighed Mrs. Armitage. "I do wish you'd learn to

be more tactful. Now we have to find somewhere else to live, and just before Christmas, too. It really is too bad."

"Do we really have to be out by eleven o'clock?" asked Mark, who, with Harriet, had been listening round-eyed.

"I shall contest it," said his father. "It's the most monstrous tyranny. They needn't think they can ride over me rough-shod."

However, Mrs. Armitage, who was a quiet but practical person, at once sent Harriet along the village to ask if they could borrow the house of Mrs. Foster, who was going off to the south of France, while they looked around for somewhere else to live. Then with the help of Agnes and Mrs. Epis she packed up all their clothes and put them in the car. Mr. Armitage refused to leave with the rest of the family, and remained behind to tackle the invaders.

At eleven o'clock sharp several men who looked like builders' laborers arrived. They rode on rather battered, paint-stained old broomsticks, and carried hammers, saws, and large sheets of beaverboard.

"Morning, Guv'ner," said one who seemed to be the foreman, advancing up the front steps.

Mr. Armitage stood in the way with his arms folded. "I protest against this unseemly intrusion!" he cried. "It is entirely contrary to the British Constitution."

"Ah," said the foreman, waving a screwdriver at him in a pitying manner, "you're cuckoo." At once Mr. Armitage vanished, and in his place a large bird flapped in a dazed manner round the front door.

Just then an enormous, sleek black car rolled silently up to the gate, and a tall, sleek, dark man stepped out and came up the steps, swinging an elegant umbrella.

"Excellent, Wantage, excellent. I see you have arrived," he said, glancing about. "I trust you have had no trouble?"

"Only a little, sir," said the foreman respectfully, indicating the bird, which let out a hoarse and indignant "Cuckoo!"

"Dear me," said the sleek gentleman. "Can this be my unfortunate friend, Mr. Armitage? Such a pleasant person— perhaps just a *little* hot-tempered, just a *little* unkind in his reviews? However, it would certainly be equally unkind to wrest him from his old home; we must find some accommodation for him. Hawkins!" The chauffeur's head looked out from the car. "Bring the case, will you."

A large glass dome was brought, of the kind which is placed over skeleton clocks, with the hours and minutes marked on one side.

"There," said the gentleman, tucking Mr. Armitage under one arm. "Now, in the study, perhaps? On one's desk, for inspiration. When I place the bird in position, Hawkins, pray cover him with the case. Thank you. A most tasteful ornament, I flatter myself, and perhaps in time we may even teach him to announce the hours."

"Your father's being a long time," said Mrs. Armitage rather anxiously to the children. "I do hope he isn't getting into trouble."

"Oh, I don't suppose it's worth expecting him before lunch," said Mark. "He'll argue with everybody and then probably go for a walk and start drafting a letter to *The Times*."

So they sat down to lunch in Mrs. Foster's house, but just as they were raising the first bites to their mouths, Harriet gave a little squeak and said:

"Goodness! We've forgotten all about Sarah! She'll arrive at the house and won't know what's happened to us."

"Oh, she's sure to see Father somewhere around, and he'll bring her along," Mark pointed out. "I wouldn't worry. We can go along afterwards and see, if they don't turn up soon."

At this moment Sarah was walking onward to her doom. She found the front door of the Armitage house open, and nobody about. This seemed to her a good moment to plant some of her practical jokes, so she opened her suitcase and stole into the dining room. The long table was already set for tea. There were thirteen places, which puzzled her, but she supposed her aunt and uncle must be giving a party. Some plates of sandwiches and cakes covered with damp napkins were standing on a side table, so she doctored them with sneezing powder, and placed fizz-bangs in some of the teacups.

She was surprised to see that the rooms had been split in two by partitions of beaverboard, and wondered where the family was, and what was going on. Hearing some hammering upstairs, she decided to tiptoe up and surprise them. Feeling around in her suitcase again, she dug out her water pistol, and charged it from a jug which stood on the sideboard. Then she went softly up the stairs.

The door facing the top of the stairs was open, and she stole through it. This was Mr. Armitage's study, which Mr. Whizzard had decided should be his private office. Just now, however, he was out having his lunch, and the room was empty. Sarah went to work at once. She laid a few thumbtacks carefully on what she supposed to be her uncle's chair, and was just attaching a neat little contrivance to the telephone, when there came an interruption. The huge black cat, Walrus, who had stayed behind when the family left, had strolled into the study after Sarah and was taking a deep interest in the dejected-looking cuckoo sitting under the glass dome. While Sarah was busy laying the thumbtacks, he leaped onto the desk, and after a moment's reflection, knocked the glass case off the desk with one sweep of his powerful paw.

"Sarah!" cried Mr. Armitage in terror, "Save me from this murdering beast!"

Completely startled, thinking that her uncle must have come in unheard while her back was turned, Sarah spun round and let fly with her water pistol. The jet caught the

unfortunate bird in mid-air, and at once (for the weather was very cold) he turned to a solid block of ice, and fell to the ground with a heavy thud. The cat pounced at once, but his teeth simply grated on the ice, and he sprang back with a hiss of dismay. **169224'7**

At that moment Mr. Whizzard returned from lunch.

"Dear me!" he said peevishly, "What is all this? Cats? Little girls? And who has been meddling with my cuckoo?" But when he saw Mr. Armitage's frozen condition, he began to laugh uncontrollably.

"Warlock! Warlock! Come and look at this," he shouted, and another man came in, wearing a mortarboard and magician's gown.

"The lads have just arrived in the dragon-bus," he said. "I told them to go straight in to tea, as the workmen haven't quite finished dividing up the classrooms. What have you got there?"

"Poor Armitage has become quite seized up," said Mr. Whizzard. "If we had a deep-freeze—"

Before he could finish, several young student-magicians dashed into the room, with cries of complaint. They were all sneezing.

"Really it's too bad, when we're all tired from our journey! Sneezing powder in everything, and tea all over the floor. A joke's a joke, but this is going too far. Someone ought to get the sack for this."

"What is the matter, my lads?" inquired Mr. Whizzard.

"Someone's been playing a lot of rotten practical jokes."

Sarah quailed and would gladly have slipped away, but she was jammed in a corner. She tried to squeeze past the desk, but one of the drawers was open and caught her suitcase. A small bomb fell out and exploded on the carpet, amid yelps of terror from the students.

"Seize that child," commanded Mr. Whizzard. Two of them unwillingly did so, and stood her before him. He cast his eye over the diabolical contents of her suitcase, and then the label attracted his attention.

"Armitage. Ah, just so, this is plainly an attempt at sabotage from the evicted family. They shall pay dearly for it. Nightshade, fetch an electric heater, will you. There's one in the front hall."

While they were waiting, Mr. Whizzard sat down in his

chair, but shot up again at once, with a murderous look at Sarah.

Nightshade returned with the heater and plugged it in.

"Good. Now place the bird before it, in this pencil tray, so as not to dampen the carpet. The cat sits at hand on this chair, ready for when the thawing process commences. It should not be long, I fancy. Now my young friends, you may return to your interrupted meal, and as for you," with a savage glance at Sarah, "a little solitary confinement will do you no harm, while I reflect on how to dispose of you."

Sarah was dragged away and locked into a beaverboard cell, which had once been part of Harriet's bedroom.

"Now I think we deserve a quiet cup of tea, after all this excitement," said Mr. Whizzard to Mr. Warlock, when they were left alone. "We can sip it as we watch poor Armitage melt. I'll ring down to the kitchen." He lifted the telephone, and instantly a flood of ink poured into his ear.

Meanwhile, Mark and Harriet had decided to come in search of their father and cousin.

"It might be wise not to go in the front way, don't you think?" said Harriet. "After all, it's rather odd that we haven't heard *something* of them by now. I feel there must have been some trouble."

So they went stealthily round through the shrubbery and climbed up the wisteria to Harriet's window. The first thing they saw when they looked in was Sarah, pacing up and down in a distracted manner.

"Good gracious—" Harriet began, but Sarah made frantic gestures to silence her. They climbed in as quietly as they could.

"Thank heaven you've come," she whispered. "Uncle Armitage is being roasted to death in the study, or else eaten by

Walrus. You must rescue him at once." They listened in horror, as she explained the position, and then hurriedly climbed out again. Sarah was no climber, so she hung out anxiously watching them, and thinking of the many times her uncle had given her half-crowns and pats on the head.

Harriet ran to the back door, where the cat's tin plate still lay, and began to rattle it, calling "Walrus, Walrus, Walrus! Dinner! Walrus! Fish!"

Mark climbed along the wisteria to the study window, to wait for the result of this move.

He saw the cat Walrus, who was still sitting on the chair, attentively watching the melting process, suddenly prick up his ears and look towards the door. Then as Harriet's voice came faintly again, he shot out of it and disappeared.

"Confound that animal!" exclaimed Mr. Whizzard. "Catch him, Warlock!" They both ran out of the door, looking to right and left. Mark wasted no time. He clambered through the window, grabbed the cuckoo, and was out again before the two men returned, frustrated and angry.

"Good heavens, now the bird's gone," cried Mr. Warlock. "What a fool you were to leave the window open. It must have flown out."

"Impossible! This is some more of that wretched child's doing. I'm going along to see her, right away."

He burst in on Sarah, looking so ferocious that she instinctively caught up the first weapon she could see, to defend herself. It was a screwdriver, left lying on the floor by one of the workmen.

"What have you done with the cuckoo?" Mr. Whizzard demanded.

"I haven't touched it," Sarah truthfully replied.

"Nonsense. Do you deny that you enticed the cat away by

black arts, and then kidnapped the cuckoo?" He approached her threateningly.

Sarah retreated as far as she could and clutched the screwdriver. "You're crackers," she said. "I tell you I haven't—" Her mouth dropped open in astonishment. For where Mr. Whizzard had been standing there was nothing but a large white cardboard box, containing red and blue paper fireworks of the kind that you pull at parties; they were decorated with silver moons and stars. At this moment Mark and Harriet came climbing back through the window.

Downstairs in the dining room the young wizards, having cleared away tea, were enjoying a singsong.

> "Ha ha ha, he he he [they sang],
> "Little broom stick, how I love thee."

They were interrupted by Mr. Warlock.

"Have any of you boys seen Mr. Whizzard?" he inquired. "He went to interview the young female prisoner, and I haven't seen him since."

"No, sir, he hasn't been in here," the eldest one said. "Won't you come and play for us, Mr. Warlock? You do play so beautifully."

"Well, just for five minutes, if you insist." They began to sing again:

> "Necromancers come away, come away, come come away,
> This is wizards' holiday,"

when suddenly they were aware of the three children, Mark, Harriet, and Sarah, standing inside the door, holding red-and-blue crackers in their hands.

"What is the meaning of this?" said Mr. Warlock severely. "You are trespassing on private property."

"Yes," said Mark. "*Our* property. This is our house, and we would like you to get out of it at once."

"Vacate it," whispered Harriet.

"Vacate it at once."

"We shall do no such thing."

"Very well then. Do you know what we have here?" he held up one of the crackers. "Your Mr. Whizzard. And if you don't get out—vacate—at once, we shall *pull* them. So you'd better hurry up."

The wizards looked at each other in consternation, and then, slowly at first, but with gathering speed, began to put their things together and take them out to the dragon coach. The children watched them, holding the crackers firmly.

"And you must take down all that beaverboard partitioning," said Harriet firmly. "I don't know *what* Mummy would say if she saw it."

"The workmen have all gone home."

"Then you must manage on your own."

The house began to resound with amateurish bangs and squeaks. "Ow, Nightshade, you clumsy clot, you dropped that board on my toe." "Well get out of the way then, you nitwit necromancer."

At last it was all done, and at the front gate the children handed over the twelve red-and-blue parts of Mr. Whizzard.

"And it's more than you deserve," said Harriet, "seeing how you were going to treat our poor Pa."

"We should also like that screwdriver, with which I perceive you have armed yourself, or we shall not be able to restore our director to his proper shape," said Mr. Warlock coldly.

"Oh, dear me, no. You're nuts if you think we're going to let you get away with that," said Sarah. "We shall want it in case of any further trouble. Besides, what about poor uncle—oh dear—" she stopped in dismay. For Mr. Warlock had disappeared, and his place had been taken by a sack of coconuts.

"Oh, never mind," said Harriet. "You didn't mean to do it. Here, do for goodness' sake hurry up and go." She shoved the sack into the arms of Nightshade, and bundled him into the coach, which slowly rolled off. "We must simply dash along to Mrs. Foster's. I'm sure Mummy will be worrying."

They burst in on Mrs. Armitage with their story. "And where is your father?" she asked immediately.

"Oh, goodness." Mark looked guilty. "I'd forgotten all about him." He carefully extracted the half-stifled cuckoo from his trouser pocket.

"Out with the screwdriver, Sarah."

Sarah obediently pointed it at him and said "You're Uncle" and he was restored to himself once more, but looking much rumpled and tattered. He glared at them all.

"I must say, that's a fine respectful way to treat your father. Carried in your trouser pocket, indeed!"

"Well, I hope this will cure you once and for all of writing those unkind reviews," said Mrs. Armitage coldly. "Now we have all the trouble of moving back again, and just when I was beginning to feel settled."

"And talking of cures," said Mr. Armitage, turning on his niece, "we won't say anything *this* time, seeing it's all turned out for the best, but if ever I catch you playing any of your practical pranks again—"

"Oh, I never, never will," Sarah assured him. "I thought people enjoyed them."

"Not in this family," said Mark.

Sweet Singeing in the Choir

"Daddy, have we really got a fairy godmother?" asked Harriet, dropping her basket full of holly leaves in a corner of the room and coming over to the fire, where tea was laid on a little table.

"Possibly, possibly," he replied, without coming out of his evening paper.

"No, but really?" she persisted. "A rather silly-looking lady, with popping eyes and a lot of necklaces?"

"Oh, yes, now I remember," said Mr. Armitage, putting down his paper and starting to laugh. "She was the one who dropped you in the font. Your mother never took to her much. And right after the christening she tried to interest me in a scheme for supplying old fairy ladies with needlework patterns."

"Goodness, can't they make their own?"

"Apparently not. Yes, of course, she was going to give you each a wish for your christening presents, but your mother pointed out that if you had it, then you'd only wish for your lunch and it might be better to wait for a few years."

"Yes, well, that's just it," exclaimed Mark. "We met her just now in Farthing Wood, and she offered us a wish each, so we said could we think it over and tell her tomorrow; you know how it is on the spur of the moment, you can never think of anything sensible."

"Very prudent of you," murmured his father. "Try not to wish for anything that needs *upkeep*, will you, like race horses or airplanes. You know what the price of gasoline is now."

Here Mrs. Armitage came in and started pouring tea.

"Children, I'm afraid I've a disappointing message for you from Mr. Pontwell. He says he's very sorry but he doesn't think he *can* have you in the carol choir."

"Not have us in the choir? But Mr. Willingdon always did."

"Well, I suppose Mr. Pontwell is more particular about voices. He says he wants the singing to be especially good this year. And you know I don't mean to be unkind, but you can neither of you sing in tune at all."

"Yes, the other day," agreed Mr. Armitage, "I wondered who could possibly be sawing wood in the bathroom, only to find—"

"Oh, he is a mean man," said Harriet, taking no notice. "*Nobody* ever minds about keeping in tune in carols. And I do love carol-singing too. Oh, why did Mr. Willingdon have to go and get made a canon?"

"Couldn't we go along with them and keep quiet?" suggested Mark.

"No, I thought of that, but he said 'You know how effervescent Mark and Harriet are, there's no knowing what they'd do.' I think he's afraid of you."

"Well, I think that's most unkind of him. We'll just have to go out by ourselves, that's all."

"No, no," said Harriet, "don't you see what we can do? What about our fairy godmother and the wishes?"

Next day, as arranged, they met the popeyed lady in Farthing Wood.

"Well, dears," she beamed at them. "Thought of a good wish?"

"Yes, please," said Mark. "We'd both like to have simply wonderful voices—to sing with, I mean."

The lady looked a little blank. "V*oices?* Are you sure you wouldn't like a nice box of chocolates each? Or a pony?"

"No, thank you very much. We have a unicorn already, you see. But we really do need good voices so that we can get into the carol choir."

"Well," she said doubtfully. "That's rather a difficult wish. I don't think I could manage it for you *permanently.* But perhaps for a week or two, I *might* be able to manage it—"

"Oh, please do try." They both looked at her imploringly.

"Very well, dears, since it means such a lot to you." She shut her eyes and clenched her fists with an appearance of terrific concentration. The children waited breathlessly.

"Now, then," she said after a moment or two, "try to sing a few notes."

They were rather embarrassed and looked at each other for encouragement.

"What shall we sing? 'Good King Wenceslas?'" They sang the first few lines rather timidly and were much disconcerted by the notes which boomed out—Harriet's voice had become a terrific contralto which would not have disgraced a twelve-stone prima donna, and Mark's was a deep, and reverend bass.

"I say, I hate to seem ungrateful, but couldn't we be soprano and treble—it would be more natural, don't you think?"

"Perhaps you are right, pettie," said the lady, and closed her eyes again, looking a shade martyred. Oh dear, we are giving her a lot of trouble, Harriet thought.

This time the result was more satisfactory, and they thanked her with heartfelt gratitude.

"How long will it last?" asked Mark.

"Thirteen days. You will find that it wears off at midnight."

"Like Cinderella," said Harriet, nodding.

"So remember not to give a performance just at that time. Well, dears, I am *so* pleased to have met you again, and please remember me to your dear Mamma."

"Oh yes, she said do drop in to tea whenever you are passing. Good-by, and thank you *so* much—you *are* kind—"

When they had left her, they dashed straight to the vicarage and inquired for Mr. Pontwell, but were told that he was round at the church.

The new vicar was a red-faced, rather pompous-looking man. He seemed slightly embarrassed at meeting Mark and Harriet.

"Oh—er, hullo, my dear children. What can I do for you?"

"Well, sir, it's about our being in the carol choir," Mark plunged.

Mr. Pontwell frowned. "Dear me, I thought I had made that perfectly plain to your dear mother. I am afraid I cannot see my way—"

"No, but," said Harriet, "we feel sure that you are acting under a wrong impression of our voices. You probably heard us on some occasion when Mark had a cold, and I was, um, suffering from my laryngitis, and of course you had quite a mistaken idea of what we could do. We just want you to be *very* kind and hear us again."

"Well really, my dear children, I don't think that is the case, and there hardly seems much point in reopening the question—however, if you insist—"

"Oh, we do insist," agreed Mark. "What shall we sing, Harriet, 'Oh, for the Wings of a Dove'?"

They were much more confident this time, and opened their mouths to their widest extent.

"Oh, for the weengs, for the weengs of a dove—
Far away, far away would I rove."

When Mr. Pontwell heard their exquisite treble voices soaring about among the rafters of the church, his eyes nearly dropped out of his head, and he sat down suddenly in a nearby pew.

"Good gracious," he said, "I had no idea—of course, you were quite right to come. My *dear* children—gracious me, what an extraordinary thing. I had quite thought—but there, it only shows how mistaken one can be. You will indeed be an addition to the choir."

He went on saying things like this as they walked through the churchyard.

"You will come to the practices on Wednesdays and Saturdays, will you?"

"Of course," said Harriet anxiously, "and when are we going out singing?"

"Monday evening, the nineteenth." Mark and Harriet did some rapid calculation. Monday the nineteenth would be the last day of their thirteen days, which seemed cutting it rather fine.

"I suppose it couldn't *possibly* be any earlier?" said Harriet. "You see, rather odd things sometimes happen to our family on Mondays—rather *unaccountable* things—and it would be so awful if we were late or prevented from coming, or anything." She was thinking of the day when their house had suddenly turned to a castle on the Rhine for twelve hours.

"No, my dear, I am afraid the date cannot be changed, as I have already made several arrangements for the evening, including a visit of the choir to Gramercy Chase. Sir Leicester will be *most* interested to hear you sing, so I do trust that you will not let any of these—er—unaccountable things happen during the day, *or* while you are out with the choir." He looked at them sternly.

"So you're really in the choir?" said Mr. Armitage that evening. "And going to Gramercy Chase. Well, well, it's a good thing it will be dark."

"Why?"

"It's the most hideous house between here and Birmingham. Sir Leicester always says he wishes he had a good excuse to pull it down. It was entirely rebuilt, you know, in nineteenth-century gothic, except for the haunted terrace."

"Haunted?" said Harriet. "Oh, good. What by? That's where we're going to sing."

"Oh, some bird, called King William's Raven (don't ask me why), who only appears to foretell bad tidings to the house of Gramercy. The last time was just before the current baronet was killed at Waterloo. He flies along the terrace lighting torches in the brackets—of course, they've put in electric lighting now, so I don't know how he'd manage—"

Harriet and Mark had a somewhat difficult time at the choir practices, as all their village friends were only too familiar with their usual voices, and they had to face a considerable amount of chaff and a lot of astonishment at this sudden development of flute-like tones.

"Been keeping quiet all these years, eh? Didn't want to waste yourselves on us, I suppose?"

"Ah," said Ruby, the blacksmith's daughter, "they've heard as how Mr. Pontwell's going to have a recording made on Monday night."

In fact, there was a general rumor going round that Mr. Pontwell had something special up his sleeve, and that was why he was so particular about the singers and the practices; though whether he was having the singing recorded, or royalty was going to be there, or some great impresario was staying at Gramercy Chase to hear them, was not known.

Mr. Pontwell made a particular point of asking them to wear tidy dark clothes and rubber-soled shoes so that they should not squeak on people's gravel.

"What a fusser he is," Mark complained to Harriet.

"Never mind," she replied. "At least we're going to be *there*."

Nothing untoward happened to Mark and Harriet on Monday the nineteenth. Indeed the day was suspiciously quiet, and they both of them became slightly anxious as evening approached. However they got away safely from home and met the other carol-singers in the vicarage at eight o'clock, as had been arranged. The vicar was handing out torches and carol books.

"Now, are we all assembled? Excellent, excellent. I suggest we start off with a good rousing 'Adeste Fideles' outside the church, just to get our lungs in, then through the village as far as Little Foldings (should take a couple of hours), where Mrs. Noakes has very kindly promised us hot drinks, and Sir Leicester is sending the station wagon to collect us all there. We are expected at Gramercy Chase round about eleven o'clock."

As they were starting on their first carol, Mark felt a cold nose pushed down his neck, and turned his head to look into the reproachful green eyes of Candleberry, their unicorn.

"Goodness! I thought you were shut up for the night. Go home, bad unicorn," he said crossly, but Candleberry shook his head.

"Dear me, is that a *unicorn?*" said Mr. Pontwell, at the end of "*Adeste Fideles.*" "He shouldn't really be here, you know."

"I'm very sorry," said Mark. "I can't think how he got out. But he's extremely well trained. He won't interrupt, and he could carry anyone who got tired."

"Very well," said Mr. Pontwell. "He certainly makes a picturesque addition. But if there's the least sign of trouble, mind, you'll have to take him home."

However, there was no trouble, though they had so many requests for encores that they arrived at Little Foldings very much behind schedule, and had to gulp down their drinks and hurry out to the station wagon, which sped away through the dark across Gramercy Wold, with the unicorn easily keeping pace beside it. Even so, they arrived at the Chase well after half-past eleven.

Sir Leicester welcomed them, and hurried them at once round to the terrace where they were to sing. Mark and Harriet tried to get a look at the hideousness of the house as they

walked past it, but only received a general impression of a lot
of pinnacles and gargoyles. The terrace was enormous—at
least half a mile long and twenty yards wide, extending to a
low wall, which was topped by a series of lampposts, now
fitted with electric lamps.

The singers, hot and panting from their hurry, flung down
coats and mufflers on the wall, and clustered together opposite the orangery door, where they were to sing. As they
were finding their places for the first carol, there was a pro-
digious clattering of hoofs, and Candleberry arrived, galloping
down the terrace like a Grand National winner. Mark went to
meet him and quiet him down. When he returned, he muttered to Harriet:

"Now I know what all the fuss was about. There are some
blokes over there in the shade with a television camera. That's
why Mr. Pontwell's been taking such a lot of trouble."

"Well, do keep an eye on Candleberry," she muttered back.
"Oh, look, here comes Mr. Pontwell. Thank goodness, now
we can start before I get nervous."

They were halfway through their first carol when Mark
noticed that Candleberry seemed very uneasy; he was shivering, stamping his feet and looking over his shoulder a great
deal. Mark himself glanced rather fearfully down the long,
dark expanse of terrace.

At the same time, Harriet heard something in her ear
that sounded like a ratchet screwdriver being painstakingly
worked into granite. She turned her head to listen and realized
that it was Mark singing. She caught hold of his hand and
tapped his watch.

"Hey," she whispered under cover of the singing, "it's midnight and we've lost our voices. Better pipe low. Bang goes our
chance of charming thousands of listeners."

Mr. Pontwell was energetically conducting "The Holly and the Ivy" when an unpleasant scent invaded his nostrils. He sniffed again—yes, it was the smell of burning clothes. Could it be that dratted unicorn, with its incandescent horn? Had it set fire to somebody's cap? He glanced about angrily, and then saw a flame leap up on the terrace wall.

"I say," called a voice through the singing, "someone's set fire to our coats!"

In fact, the pile of coats and scarves was now blazing up in a positive bonfire.

Instantly there was a clamor of angry voices, and the singing died away.

"Ladies—gentlemen—my dear friends," cried Mr. Pontwell in anguish, "please—the evening will be ruined—"

"It's that perishing unicorn," someone exclaimed furiously. "—Never ought to have been allowed to come—"

But at that moment Candleberry came galloping in hot pursuit of something which was flying along the terrace carrying a light. As they passed through the illumination of the bonfire this was seen to be an enormous dark bird carrying a lighted candle, the flame of which streamed over its shoulder.

"Good heavens," cried Sir Leicester, who had gone very pale, "it's the family raven."

"Please, my dear singers," implored Mr. Pontwell, who thought of nothing but his performance, "let us have a little order. What do a few coats and scarves matter? Or a little natural fauna? Let me hear a nice spirited rendering of 'We Three Kings'."

But at that moment a man dashed towards them from the television camera, crying: "Bring that unicorn back. It's miraculous! A real unicorn, chasing a ghostly raven—good Lord, this will be the television scoop of the century! Stand back, will you! Who owns the unicorn? You sir? Can you get him to come this way?"

Mark called Candleberry, and the unicorn galloped back, driving the raven in front of him. It was still crossly looking for something to light with its candle. It had been foiled by the electric lamps and had to fall back on the heap of coats. At last with a croak of decision it swooped down and set fire to somebody's carol book.

"Stop it, stop it," shrieked Mr. Pontwell, but the TV expert at the same moment shouted "Hold it, hold it. Stand aside, you others. Hold out your books. This is wonderful, wonderful!"

Only Mr. Pontwell was not pleased with the evening's work. Everyone else was warmed and exhilarated by the fire and informed that their fees as television performers would amply cover the loss of coats and carol books. Sir Leicester himself seemed to have disappeared, but his chauffeur drove the choir back, cheerful and chattering, at about three in the morning.

"Poor man," said Harriet to Mark, "I expect he's worrying about what dreadful doom is going to fall on the House of Gramercy. After all, it's not so funny for him."

At breakfast next morning the telephone rang. Mr. Armitage answered it, and after listening for a few minutes, began to laugh.

"It was Sir Leicester," he said, returning to the table. "He's had his dreadful doom. The architect's report on Gramercy Chase has come in, and he's learned that the whole place is riddled with dry rot. It's all got to come down. He's simply delighted. He rang up to ask if I knew of a comfortable cottage for sale."

Harriet's Hairloom

"Oh, Mother," Harriet said, as she did every year, "can't I open my birthday presents at breakfast?"

"Certainly not! You know perfectly well that you weren't born till half past four. You get your birthday presents at teatime, not before."

"We could change the custom now we're in our teens," Harriet suggested cunningly. "You know you hate having to get up at half past two in the morning for Mark's presents."

But Mark objected strongly to any change, and Mrs. Armitage added, "In any case, don't forget that as it's your thirteenth birthday, you have to be shown into the Closed Room; there'd never be time to do that before school. Go and collect your schoolbooks now, and, Mark, wash the soot from behind your ears; if you must hunt for Lady Anne's pearls in the chimney, I wish you'd clean up before coming to breakfast."

"You'd be as pleased as anyone else if I found them," Mark answered.

Later, as he and Harriet walked to the school bus, Mark said, "I think it's a rotten swindle that only girls in the family are allowed to go inside the Closed Room when they get to be thirteen. Suppose there's a monster like at Glamis, what'll you do?"

"Tame it," said Harriet promptly. "I shall feed it on bread-and-milk and lettuce."

"That's hedgehogs, dope! Suppose it has huge teeth and tentacles and a poisonous sting three yards long?"

"Shut up! Anyway I don't suppose it is a monster. It would have starved long ago. It's probably just some moldering old great aunt in her coffin or something boring like that."

Still, it was nice to have a Closed Room in the family, Harriet reflected, and she sat in the bus happily speculating about what it might contain—jewels, perhaps, rubies as big as tomatoes; or King Arthur's sword, Excalibur, left with the Armitage family for safekeeping when he went off to Avalon; or the Welsh bard Taliesin, fallen asleep in the middle of a poem; or a cockatrice; or the vanished crew of the *Marie Celeste*, playing cards and singing shanties. . . .

Harriet was still in a dreamy state when school began. The first lesson was Geography with old Mr. Gubbins so there was no need to pay attention; she sat trying to think of suitable pet names for cockatrices until she heard a stifled sobbing on her left.

". . . is of course the Cathay of the ancients," Mr. Gubbins was rambling on. "Marco Polo in his travels . . ."

Harriet looked cautiously around and saw that her best friend and left-hand neighbor, Desiree, or Dizzry as everyone called her, was crying bitterly, hunched over the inkwell on her desk so that the tears ran into it.

Dizzry was the daughter of Ernie Perrow, the village chimney-sweep; the peculiarity of the Perrow family was that none of them ever grew to be more than six inches high. Instead of sitting at her desk in the usual way Dizzry sat on top of it, at a small table and chair which Mark had obligingly made for her out of matchboxes.

"What's the matter?" whispered Harriet. "Here, don't cry into the ink—you'll make it weaker than it is already. Haven't you a handkerchief?"

She pulled sewing things out of her own desk, snipped a shred off the corner of a tablecloth she was embroidering, and passed it to Dizzry, who gulped, nodded, took a deep breath, and wiped her eyes on it.

"What's the matter?" Harriet asked again.

"It was what Mr. Gubbins said that started me off," Dizzry muttered. "Talking about Cathay. Our Min always used to say she'd a fancy to go to Cathay. She'd got it muddled up with *café*. She thought she'd get cake and raspberry ade and ice cream there."

"Well, so what?" said Harriet, who saw nothing to cry about in that.

"Haven't you heard? We've lost her—we've lost our Min!"

"Oh, my goodness! You mean she's died?"

"No, not *died*. Just lost. Nobody's seen her since yesterday breakfast time!"

Harriet privately thought this ought to have been rather a relief for the family but was too polite to say so. Min, the youngest of the Perrow children, was a perfect little fiend, always in trouble of one kind or another. When not engaged in entering sweet jars in the village shop and stealing Butter Kernels or Quince Drops, she was probably worming her way through keyholes and listening to people's secrets, or hitching a free lift round the houses in the postman's pocket and jabbing him with a darning needle as a reward for the ride, or sculling about the pond on Farmer Beezeley's ducks and driving them frantic by tickling them under their wings, or galloping down the street on somebody's furious collie, or climbing into the vicar's TV and frightening him half to death by shouting, "Time is short!" through the screen. She frequently ran fearful risks but seemed to have a charmed life. Everybody in the village heartily detested Min Perrow, but her older brothers and sisters were devoted to her and rather proud of her exploits.

Poor Dizzry continued to cry, on and off, for the rest of the day. Harriet tried to console her but it seemed horridly probable that Min had at last gone too far and been swallowed by a cow or drowned in a sump or rolled into a Swiss roll at the bakery while stealing jam—so many ill fates might easily have befallen her that it was hard to guess the likeliest.

"I'll help you hunt for her this evening," Harriet promised, however, "and so will Mark. As soon as my birthday tea's finished."

Dizzry came home with Harriet for the birthday tea and was a little cheered by the cake, made in the shape of a penguin with black-currant icing and an orange beak, and by Harriet's presents, which included a do-it-yourself water-divining kit from Mark (a hazel twig and a bucket of water), an electronic guitar which could sing as well as play, a little pocket computer for working out sums, and from the children's fairy godmother a tube of endless toothpaste. Harriet

was not particularly grateful for this last; the thought of toothpaste supplied for the rest of her life left her unmoved.

"I'd rather have had an endless stick of licorice," she said crossly. "Probably I shan't have any teeth left by the time I'm ninety; what use will toothpaste be then?"

Her presents from Dizzry were by far the nicest: a pink-and-orange necklace of spindleberries, beautifully carved, and a starling named Alastair whom Dizzry had trained to take messages, answer the telephone or the front door, and carry home small quantities of shopping. (At first Harriet was a little anxious about Walrus the cat's reactions to this new member of the household, and indeed Walrus was somewhat aggressive, but Harriet found she had no need to worry: Alastair had also been trained to defend himself against cats, and Walrus soon learned to keep his paws to himself.)

"Now," said Mrs. Armitage rather nervously when the presents had been admired, "I'd better show Harriet the Closed Room."

Mr. Armitage hurriedly retired to his study while Mark, controlling some natural feelings of envy, kindly said he would help Dizzry hunt for Min, and carried her off to inspect all the reapers and binders in Mr. Beezeley's farmyard.

Harriet and Mrs. Armitage went up to the attic, and Mrs. Armitage paused before a cobweb-shrouded door and pulled a rusty old key out of her pocket.

"Now you must say, 'I, Harriet Armitage, solemnly swear not to reveal the secret of this room to any other soul in the world.'"

"But when I grow up and have a daughter," objected Harriet, "won't I have to tell her, just as Great Aunt Charlotte told you and you're telling me?"

"Well, yes, I suppose so," Mrs. Armitage said uncertainly.

"I've rather forgotten how the oath went, to tell you the truth."

"Why do we have to promise not to tell?"

"To be honest, I haven't the faintest idea."

"Let's skip that bit—there doesn't seem much point to it—and just go in," Harriet suggested. So they opened the door (it was very stiff, for it had been shut at least fifteen years) and went in.

The attic was dim, lit only through a patch of green glass tiles in the roof; it was quite empty except for a small, dusty loom, made of black wood with a stool to match.

"A loom?" said Harriet, very disappointed. "Is *that* all?"

"It isn't an ordinary loom," her mother corrected her. "It's a hairloom. For weaving human hair."

"Who wants to weave human hair? What can you make?"

"I suppose you make a human hair mat. You must only use hair that's never been cut since birth."

"Haven't you tried?"

"Oh my dear, I never seemed to get a chance. By the time your father's Aunt Charlotte showed me the loom everyone was wearing their hair short; you couldn't get a piece long enough to weave for love or money. And then you children came along—somehow I never found time."

"Well I jolly well shall," Harriet said. "I'll try and get hold of some hair. I wonder if Miss Pring would let me have hers? I bet it's never been cut—she must have yards. Maybe you can make a cloak of invisibility, or the sort that turns swans into humans."

Harriet was so pleased with this notion that only as they went downstairs did she think to ask, "How did the loom get into the family?"

"I'm a bit vague about that," Mrs. Armitage admitted. "I

believe it belonged to a Greek ancestress that one of the crusading Armitages married and brought back to England. She's the one your middle name is Penelope after."

Without paying much attention, Harriet went off to find Mark and Dizzry. Her father said they had gone along to the church, so she followed, pausing at the post office to ask elderly Miss Pring, the postmistress, if she would sell her long gray hair to be woven into a rug.

"It would look very pretty," Harriet coaxed. "I could dye some of it pink or blue."

Miss Pring was not keen.

"Sell my hair? Cut it off? The idea! *Dye* it? What impertinence! Get along with you, saucebox!"

So Harriet had to abandon that scheme, but she stuck a postcard on the notice board: HUMAN HAIR REQUIRED, UNCUT; BEST PRICES PAID, and posted another to the local paper. Then she joined Mark and Dizzry, who were searching the church organ pipes for Min, but without success.

Harriet had met several other members of the Perrow family on her way: Ernie, Min's father, driving an old dolls' pushchair which he had fitted with an engine and turned into a convertible like a Model T Ford; old Gran Perrow, stomping along and gloomily shouting "Min!" down all the drainholes; and Sid, one of the boys, riding a bike made from cocoa tins and poking out nests from the hedges with a bamboo stick in case Min had been abducted.

When it was too dark to go on searching, Harriet and Mark left Dizzry at Rose Cottage, where the Perrows lived.

"We'll go on looking tomorrow!" they called. And Harriet said, "Don't worry too much."

"I expect she'll be all right wherever she is," Mark said. "I'd back Min against a mad bull any day."

As they walked home he asked Harriet, "What about the Closed Room, then? Any monster?"

"No, very dull, just a hairloom."

"I say, you shouldn't tell me, should you?"

"It's all right—we agreed to skip the promise to keep it secret."

"What a letdown," Mark said. "Who wants an old loom?"

They arrived home to trouble. Their father was complaining, as he did every day, about soot on the carpets and black tidemarks on the bathroom basin and towels.

"Well if you don't *want* me to find Lady Anne's necklace—" Mark said aggrievedly. "If it was worth a thousand pounds when she lost it in 1660, think what it would fetch now."

"Why in heaven's name would it be up the *chimney*? Stop arguing and go to bed. And brush your teeth!"

"I'll lend you some of my toothpaste," Harriet said.

"Just the same," Mark grumbled, brushing his teeth with yards of toothpaste so that the foam stood out on either side of his face like Dundreary whiskers and flew all over the bathroom, "Ernie Perrow definitely told me that his great-great-great-grandfather, Oliver Perrow, had a row with Lady Anne Armitage because she ticked him off for catching field mice in her orchard; Oliver was the village sweep, and her pearls vanished just after that; Ernie thinks old Oliver stuck them in the chimney to teach her a lesson, and then he died, eaten by a fox before he had a chance to tell anyone. But Ernie's sure that's where the pearls are."

"Perhaps Min's up there looking for them too."

"Not her! She'd never do anything as useful as that."

Harriet had asked Alastair the starling to call her at seven; in fact, she was roused at half past six by loud bangs on the front door.

"For heaven's sake, somebody tell that maniac to go away!" shouted Mr. Armitage from under his pillow.

Harriet flung on a dressing gown and ran downstairs. What was her surprise to find at the door a little old man in a white duffel coat with the hood up. He carried a very large parcel, wrapped in sacking. Harriet found the sharp look he gave her curiously disconcerting.

"Would it be Miss Armitage now, the young lady who put the advertisement in the paper then?"

"About hair?" Harriet said eagerly. "Yes, I did. Have you got some, Mr.—?"

"Mr. Thomas Jones the Druid, I am. Beautiful hair I have then, look you—finer than any lady's in the land. Only see now till I get this old parcel undone!" And he dumped the bundle down at her feet and started unknotting the cords. Harriet helped. When the last half-hitch twanged apart, a great springy mass of hair came boiling out. It was soft and fine, dazzlingly white, with just a few strands of black, and smelled slightly of tobacco.

"There, now, indeed to goodness! Did you ever see finer?"

"But," said Harriet, "has it ever been cut short?" She very much hoped that it had not; it seemed impossible that they would ever be able to parcel it up again.

"Never has a scissor blade been laid to it, till I cut it all off last night," the old man declared.

Harriet wondered whose it was; something slightly malicious and self-satisfied about the old man's grin as he said "I cut it all off" prevented her from asking.

"Er—how much would you want for it?" she inquired cautiously.

"Well, indeed," he said. "It would be hard to put a price on such beautiful hair, whatever."

At this moment there came an interruption. A large van drew up in front of the Armitage house. On its sides iridescent bubbles were painted, and, in rainbow colors, the words SUGDEN'S SOAP.

A uniformed driver jumped out, consulting a piece of paper.

"Mr. Mark Armitage live here?" he asked Harriet. She nodded.

"Will he take delivery of one bathroom, complete with shower, tub, footbath, deluxe basin, plastic curtains, turkish towels, chrome sponge-holder, steel-and-enamel hairdryer, and a six years' supply of Sugden's Soap?"

"I suppose so," Harriet said doubtfully. "You're sure there's no mistake?"

The delivery note certainly had Mark's name and address on it.

"Mark!" Harriet yelled up the stairs, forgetting it was still only seven A.M. "Did you order a bathroom? Because it's come."

"Merciful goodness!" groaned the voice of Mr. Armitage. "Has *no* one any consideration for my hours of rest?"

Mark came running down, looking slightly embarrassed.

"Darn it," he said as he signed the delivery note, "I never expected I'd get a *bathroom:* I was hoping for the free cruise to Saposoa."

"Where shall we put it, Guv?" said the driver, who was plainly longing to go away and get some breakfast at the nearest truck-drivers' pull-up.

Mark looked about him vaguely. At this moment Mr. Armitage came downstairs in pajamas and a very troublesome frame of mind.

"Bathroom? Bathroom?" he said. "You've bought a bathroom? What the blazes did you want to go and get a bathroom for? Isn't the one we have good enough for you, pray? You leave it dirty enough. Who's going to pay for this? And why has nobody put the kettle on?"

"I won it," Mark explained, blushing. "It was the second prize in the Sugden's Soap competition. In the *Radio Times*, you know."

"What did you have to do?" Harriet asked.

"Ten uses for soap in correct order of importance."

"I bet *washing* came right at the bottom," growled his father. "Greased stairs and fake soft centers in chocolates are more your mark."

"Anyway he won!" Harriet pointed out. "Was that all you had to do?"

"You had to write a couplet too."

"What was yours?"

Mark blushed even pinker. "Rose or White or Heliotrope, Where there's life there's Sugden's Soap."

"Come on now," said the truck driver patiently. "We don't want to be here all day, do we? Where shall we put it, Guv? In the garden?"

"Certainly not," snapped Mr. Armitage. He was proud of his garden.

"How about in the field?" suggested Harriet diplomatically. "Then Mark and I can wash in it, and you needn't be upset by soot on the towels."

"That's true," her father said, brightening a little. "All right, stick it in the field. And now will somebody *please* put on a kettle and make a cup of tea, is that too much to ask?"

And he stomped back to bed, leaving Mark and the driver to organize the erection of the bathroom in the field beside the house. Harriet put a kettle on the stove and went back to Mr. Jones the Druid who was sunning himself on the front porch.

"Have you decided what you want for your hair?" she asked.

"Oh," he said. "There is a grand new bathroom you have with you! Lucky that is, indeed. Now I am thinking I do not want any money at all for my fine bundle of hair, but only to strike a bargain with you."

"Very well," Harriet said cautiously.

"No bathroom I have at my place, see? Hard it is to wash the old beard, and chilly of a winter morning in the stream. But if you and your brother, that I can see is a kindhearted obliging young gentleman, would let me come and give it a bit of a lather now and again in *your* bathroom—"

"Why, yes, of course," Harriet said. "I'm sure Mark won't mind at all."

"So it shall be, then. Handy that will be, indeed. Terrible deal of the old beard there is, look you, and grubby she do get."

With that he undid his duffel coat and pulled back the hood. All around his head and wound about his body like an Indian sari was a prodigiously long white beard which he proceeded to untwine until it trailed on the ground. It was similar to the white hair in the bundle, but not so clean.

"Is that somebody's beard, then?" Harriet asked, pointing to the bundle.

"My twin brother, Dai Jones the Bard. Bathroom he has by him, the lucky old *cythryblwr!* But soon I will be getting a bigger one. Made a will, my dad did, see, leaving all his money to the one of us who has the longest and whitest beard on our ninetieth birthday; that falls tomorrow on Mid-

summer Day. So I crept into his house last night and cut his beard off while he slept; hard he'll find it now to grow another beard in time! All Dada's money I will be getting, he, he, he!"

Mr. Jones the Druid chuckled maliciously.

Harriet could not help thinking he was rather a wicked old man, but a bargain was a bargain, so she picked up the bundle of beard, with difficulty, and was about to say good-by when he stopped her.

"Weaving the hair into a mat, you would be, isn't it?" he said wheedlingly. "There is a fine bath mat it would make! Towels and curtains there are in the grand new bathroom of yours but no bath mat—pity that is, indeed." He gave her a cunning look out of the corner of his eyes, but Harriet would not commit herself.

"Come along this evening, then, I will, for a good old wash-up before my birthday," Mr. Jones said. He wound himself in his beard again and went off with many nods and bows. Harriet ran to the field to see how the bathroom was getting on. Mark had it nearly finished. True enough, there was no bath mat. It struck Harriet that Mr. Jones's suggestion was not a bad one.

"I'll start weaving a mat as soon as we've had another thorough hunt for Min Perrow," she said. "Saturday, thank goodness, no school."

However, during breakfast (which was late, owing to various events) Ernie Perrow drove along in the pushchair with Lily and Dizzry to show the Armitages an air-letter which had arrived from the British Consul in Cathay.

Dear Sir or Madam,
 Kindly make earliest arrangements to send passage money back to England for your daughter Hermione

who has had herself posted here, stowed away in a
box of Health Biscuits. Please forward without delay fare and expenses totaling £1,093. 7s.1d.

A postscript, scrawled by Min, read: "Dun it at larst! Nutts
to silly old postmun!"

"Oh, what shall we do?" wept Mrs. Perrow. "A thousand
pounds! How can we ever find it?"

While the grown-ups discussed ways and means to raise
the money, Mark went back to his daily search for Lady
Anne's pearls, and Harriet took the woebegone Dizzry up to
the attic, hoping to distract her by a look at the hairloom.

Dizzry was delighted with it. "Do let's do some weaving!"
she said. "I like weaving better than anything."

So Harriet lugged in the great bundle of beard, and they set
up the loom. Dizzry was an expert weaver. She had been making beautiful scarves for years on a child's toy loom. She
could nip to and fro with the shuttle almost faster than Harriet's eyes could follow. By teatime they had woven a handsome thick white mat with the words "Bath Ma" across the
middle (there had not been quite enough black for the final
T).

"Anyway you can see what it's meant to be," Harriet said.
They took the new mat and spread it in their elegant bathroom.

"Tell you what," Mark said, "we'd better hide the bath and
basin plugs when Min gets back or she'll climb in and drown
herself."

"Oh, I do wonder what Dad and Mum are doing about
getting her back," sighed Dizzry, who was sitting on a sponge.
She wiped her eyes on a corner of Harriet's facecloth.

"Let's go along to your house," Harriet said, "and find out."

There was an atmosphere of deep gloom in the Perrow household. Ernie had arranged to sell his Model T pushchair, the apple of his eye, to the Motor Museum at Beaulieu.

"A thousand pound they say they'll give for it," he said miserably. "With that and what I've saved from the chimney sweeping, we can just about pay the fare. Won't I half clobber young Min when I get her back, the little varmint!"

"Mrs. Perrow," Harriet said, "may Dizzry come and spend the evening at our house, as Mother and Daddy are going to a dance? And have a bath in our new bathroom? Mother says it's all right and I'll take great care of her."

"Oh, very well, if your Ma doesn't mind," sighed Mrs. Perrow. "I'm so distracted I hardly know if I'm coming or going. Don't forget your wash things, Diz, and the bathsalts."

Harriet was enchanted with the bathsalts, no bigger than hundreds-and-thousands. On Midsummer Eve the Armitage children were allowed to stay up as late as they liked. Mark, a single-minded boy, said he intended to go on hunting for Lady Anne's necklace in the chimney. The girls had their baths and then went up to Harriet's room with a bagful of apples and the gramophone, intending to have a good gossip.

At half past eleven Harriet, happening to glance out of the window, saw a light in the field.

"That must be Mr. Jones," she said. "I'd forgotten he was coming to shampoo his beard. It's not Mark, I can still hear him bumping around in the chimney."

There was indeed an excited banging to be heard from the chimney-breast, but it was as nothing compared with the terrible racket that suddenly broke out in the field. They heard shouts and cries of rage, thuds, crashes, and the tinkle of smashed glass.

"Heavens, what can be going on?" cried Harriet. She flung up the sash and prepared to climb out of the window.

"Wait for me!" cried Dizzry.

"Here, jump into my pocket. Hold tight!"

Harriet slid down the wisteria and dashed across the garden. A moment later they arrived at the bathroom door and witnessed a wild scene.

Evidently, Mr. Jones the Druid had finished washing his beard and had been about to leave when he saw his doom waiting for him outside the door in the form of another, very angry old man who was trying to batter his way in.

"It must be his brother!" Harriet whispered. "Mr. Jones the Bard!"

The second old man had no beard, only a ragged white frill cut short round his chin. He was shouting:

"Wait till I catch you, you *hocsdwr*, you *herwhaliwr*, you *ffrawddunio*, you wicked old *llechwr*! A snake would think shame to spit on you! Cutting off your brother's beard, indeed! Just let me get at you and I'll trim you to spillikins, I'll shave your beard round your eyebrows!" And he beat on the door with a huge pair of shears. A pane of glass fell in and broke on the bathroom tiles; then the whole door gave way.

Dizzry left Harriet's pocket and swarmed up onto her head to see what was happening. They heard a fearful bellow from inside the bathroom, a stamping and crashing, fierce grunts, the hiss of the shower, and more breaking glass.

"Hey!" Harriet shouted. "Stop wrecking our bathroom!"

No answer. The noise of battle went on.

Then the bathroom window flew open, and Jones the Druid shot out, all tangled in his beard, which was snowy white now, but still damp. He had the bath mat rolled up under his arm.

As soon as he was out, he flung it down, leaped on it, and shouted, "Take me out of here!"

The mat took off vertically and hovered, about seven feet up, while Jones the Druid began hauling in his damp beard, hand over hand.

"Come back!" Harriet cried. "You've no right to go off with our bath mat."

Jones the Bard came roaring out of the window, waving his shears.

"Come back, *ystraffaldiach!* Will you come down off there and let me mince you into macaroni! Oh, you wicked old weasel, I'll trim your beard shorter than an earwig's toe-nails!"

He made a grab for the bath mat, but it was just out of reach.

"He, he, he!" cackled Jones the Druid up above. "You didn't know your fine beard would make up so nice into a flying carpet, did you, Brother? Has to be woven on a hair-loom on Midsummer Eve and then it'll carry you faster than the Aberdovey Flyer."

"Just let me get at you, *rheibiwr!*" snarled Jones the Bard, making another vain grab.

But Dizzry, who was now jumping up and down on the top of Harriet's head, made a tremendous spring, grabbed hold of a trailing strand of Jones the Druid's beard, and hauled herself up onto a corner of the flying bath mat.

"O dammo!" gasped the Druid at sight of her. He was so taken aback that he lost his balance, staggered, and fell head-long on top of his brother. There was a windmill confusion of arms and legs, all swamped by the foaming mass of beard. Then Jones the Bard grabbed his shears with a shout of tri-umph and began chopping away great swags of white hair.

Harriet, however, paid no attention to these goings-on.

"Dizzry!" she shouted, cupping her hands round her mouth. "It's a wishing-mat. Make it take you—"

Dizzry nodded. She needed no telling. "Take me to Cathay!" she cried, and the mat soared away through the milky air of Midsummer Night.

At this moment Mark came running across the field.

"Oh, Mark!" Harriet burst out. "Look what those old fiends have done to our bathroom! It's ruined! They ought to be made to pay for it."

Mark glanced through the broken window. The place was certainly a shambles: bath and basin were both smashed, the sponge rack was wrapped round the hairdryer, the towels were trodden into a soggy pulp, and the curtains were in ribbons.

The Jones brothers were in equally bad shape. Jones the Bard was kneeling on Jones the Druid's stomach; he had managed to trim every shred of hair off his brother's head, but he himself was as bald as a coot. Both had black eyes and swollen lips.

"Oh well," Mark said. "They seem to have trouble of their own. I bet neither of them comes into that legacy now. And I never did care much for washing anyway. Look, here comes Dizzry back."

The bath mat swooped to a threepoint landing; Dizzry and Min rolled off it, laughing and crying.

"You wicked, wicked, bad little girl," Dizzry cried, shaking and hugging her small sister at the same time. "Don't you ever dare do such a thing again!"

"Now I will take my own property which is my lawful beard," said Mr. Jones the Bard, and he jumped off his brother's stomach onto the mat and addressed it in a flood of

Welsh, which it evidently understood, for it rose into the air and flew off in a westerly direction. Mr. Jones the Druid slunk away across the field looking, Dizzry said, as hangdog as a cat that has fallen into the milk.

"Now we've lost our bath mat," Harriet sighed.

"I'll help you make another," Dizzry said. "There's plenty of hair lying about. And at least we've got Min back."

"Was it nice in Cathay, Min?" Mark asked.

"Smashing. I had rice cake and cherry ice and Coca-Cola."

At this point Mr. and Mrs. Armitage returned from their dance and kindly drove Dizzry and Min home to break the joyful news to their parents.

Harriet and Mark had a try at putting the bathroom to rights, but it was really past hope.

"I must say, trouble certainly haunts this household," remarked Mr. Armitage, when he came back and found them at it. "Hurry up and get to bed, you two. Do you realize it's four o'clock on Midsummer Morning? Oh, Lord, I suppose now we have to go back to the old regime of sooty footmarks all over the bathroom."

"Certainly not," said Mark. "I'd forgotten to tell you. I found Lady Anne's pearls."

He pulled them out and dangled them: a soot-black, six-foot double strand of pearls as big as cobnuts, probably worth a king's ransom.

"Won't Ernie Perrow be pleased to know they really were in the chimney?" he said.

"Oh, go to bed!" snapped his father. "I'm fed up with hearing about the Perrows."

The Ghostly Governess

The house stood a little way above the town, on the side of a hill. The front windows looked out on a great bare expanse of downs, stretching into the distance. From the pantry, and the bathroom, and the window halfway up the stairs, you could see down the river valley to Lynchbourne, the smoky port two miles away, and beyond its roofs, masts, and funnels was the silver line of the sea.

The children approved of the house at once; it was old and full of unexpected corners, with a smell of polished floors and lavender and old carpets. The family had taken it furnished for August.

"I asked the agent and he said we could use the piano," said Mrs. Armitage, "so you'll be able to keep up with your practicing."

But Mark and Harriet made secret faces at each other. They preferred the idea of hide-and-seek in the unexplored cupboards or picnics on the downs, or taking a boat down the river to the sea. They also explored the town—it was hardly more than a village—below the house. The thing they liked best was a cottage down by the river. The paths in its gardens were all paved with oyster shells, and there were two great carved dolphins on either side of the door.

"I wonder who lives there," said Mark. "I bet they've got some lovely things inside."

But the cottage seemed to be unoccupied. The windows were all closed and curtained, and no smoke came from the chimney. They found out that it belonged to an admiral, so it seemed probable that he was at sea.

By the end of a week they felt as if they had been there all their lives. Every day they asked if they could take out a picnic lunch, and the Armitage parents declared that they had never known such peace; they hardly saw the children from breakfast till supper time.

"But I'm glad to find that you're keeping up your practicing," said Mrs. Armitage, "I heard you playing that little German tune—what is it?—'Du Lieber Augustin'—very nicely the other evening."

"Oh, yes," said Harriet, and looked blank. The conversation turned on other things. Afterwards when she compared notes with Mark they agreed that neither of them had ever played "Du Lieber Augustin."

"Do you suppose Father might have?"

"He never plays anything but Bach and Beethoven."

"Well, someone must have played it, because I was humming it this morning, so I must have heard it somewhere."

"Maybe it was on the wireless. Let's take our bikes down to Lynchbourne and see if there's a new ship in."

They forgot about the incident, but later Harriet had cause to remember it. She woke in the night very thirsty, and found that her glass was empty. Coming back from the bathroom, she thought she heard a noise downstairs and paused. Could someone be playing the piano at half past one in the morning? Harriet was not at all timid, and she resolved to go and see. She stole down the stairs in her slippers. Yes, there it was again—a faint thread of melody. She pushed the drawing-room door open and looked in.

The moon was setting and threw long stripes of light across the floor and the polished lid of the grand piano. There was nobody in the room. But as Harriet stood in the doorway she heard faint tinkling music which sounded more like a cottage piano than a Bechstein, and after a moment a quavering old voice was lifted in song:

"*Ach, du lieber Augustin, Weib ist hin, Gold ist hin,*
Ach, du lieber Augustin, alles ist hin".

The piano keys were moving up and down by themselves.

Harriet ought to have been terribly frightened, but she was not. The quavering voice sounded too harmless. She stood in fascination, watching the keys move and wondering how long it would go on, and if, perhaps, she were dreaming.

Presently the music stopped, and there was the sound of the stool being pushed back. Harriet took a step backwards. On the edge of the patch of moonlight she saw a little, frail old woman, dressed in a long gray skirt, white starched blouse, and a gray shawl over her shoulders.

"Ah," she said in a brisk, but kind voice, "you don't know

me yet, child, I am your new governess. Come, come, where are your manners? I should see a nice curtsy."

"How do you do," said Harriet, curtsying automatically.

"I hope we shall get along very well," the old lady continued. "Strict but kind is my motto, and *always* ladylike behavior. If you want an example of *that*, you have only to look up to our dear queen, who is such a pattern of all the virtues."

"Yes," said Harriet absently, looking at her enormous cameo brooch, velvet neckband and elastic-sided boots. The governess reminded her of the old yellow photographs in her grandmother's house.

"But now, child," said the old lady, "you must be going for your afternoon rest. It is nearly two o'clock. Later we shall begin to know each other better. By the way, I have not yet told you my name. It is Miss Allison. Now run along, and don't let me find you chattering to your brother during the rest hour."

"No, Miss Allison," said Harriet mechanically, and such was the governess' spell over her that she turned round and did indeed go straight back to bed and to sleep.

Next morning at breakfast Harriet was silent, as if stunned. However, her father and brother talked all the time, and her silence was not noticed.

Later, when she and Mark were sitting in a quarry, eating the eleven o'clock instalment of their lunch (chocolate and buns) Mark said:

"What's happened to you? Toothache?"

"No. Mark," said Harriet unexpectedly. "Do you remember the other day when Mother said something about my practicing 'Lieber Augustin,' and I hadn't, and we thought it must have been the wireless?"

"Yes."

"Well, I think we've got a ghost in the house." And she told him the story of her last night's adventure.

Odd events were not uncommon in the Armitage family, so Mark did not, as many brothers would have done, say, "Rats, you're trying to pull my leg." He sat reflecting for a while. Then he said: "What did you say her name was?"

"Miss Allison."

"And she was dressed in a sort of Victorian costume?"

"Yes. I don't know what sort of time exactly—it might be anything from 1840 to 1900 I should think," said Harriet vaguely, "but, oh yes, she did say something about looking up to our dear queen as a pattern of propriety. It sounded like Queen Victoria."

"I do hope we see her again," said Mark. "It sounds as if her day and night were the exact opposite of ours, if she told you to go and rest at two in the morning."

Harriet agreed with this. "And another thing," she said, "I believe she's only visible in the complete dark. Because at first she was sitting in the moonlight playing the piano—at least I suppose she was—and I couldn't see her at all till she stepped out of the light into the darkness."

"Well, well, we'll have to start picketing her. I suppose she gets up when it gets dark."

"Nonsense," said Harriet, "that wouldn't be till after ten. You never heard of a governess getting up at ten, did you? No, I bet she gets up in the *light*, just as we get up in the dark in winter."

"Anyway we'll have to have one of us watching for her at night," Mark went on. "We'll have to do it in shifts and get some sleep in the daytime. We'd better start now."

"Let's have lunch first."

So they ate their picnic and then dutifully lay back on the

springy turf and closed their eyes. But it was not a great success, for one or the other of them kept bouncing up with
brilliant ideas on ghost-governesses. They agreed that it would
be best if they both watched together the first night in case
she turned out not to be the mild inoffensive creature that
she had appeared to Harriet. They also agreed to take pencils
and notebooks with them, in case she took advantage of her
governess-hood and started teaching. Besides, they might
learn something interesting.

At last they did achieve an intermittent doze, in the hot
sun and the silence, and lay there for a couple of hours. Then
they picked an enormous basketful of cowslips and started
home for a late tea.

That night they listened carefully until the parents had
gone to bed, and then slipped downstairs into the drawing-
room. As before, the moonlight lay across the floor, but much
farther round. Everything was silent, and all they could hear
was their own breathing. Harriet began to have a dreadful
feeling of disappointment.

"Perhaps she won't come again," she whispered gloomily.

"Nonsense," said Mark, "we've hardly been here any time.
If your feet are cold, sit in the armchair and tuck them under
you."

Harriet thought this a good idea. They sat on, and now they
could hear the grandfather clock ticking in the hall, and the
lonely lowing of a cow somewhere below in the valley.

All of a sudden a quiet voice said: "Ah! Children. There
you are. I've been looking for you everywhere. This, Harriet,
is your brother Mark, I presume?"

Harriet's heart gave a violent jump, and then began beating very quickly. Miss Allison was standing, as she had been
yesterday, on the edge of the pool of moonlight. She held a

ruler in her hand and looked benevolent, but just slightly impatient.

Harriet got up and curtsied, and then she introduced Mark, who was standing with his mouth open, but otherwise looked fairly collected.

"Now we will go to the schoolroom," said the governess, "and that is where I should like you to wait for me in future. We will only come to the drawing-room for music lessons on Tuesdays and Fridays."

The children cast anxious glances at each other, but followed her upstairs meekly enough, watching with interest as she twinkled in and out of patches of moonlight in the corridor, and wondering which room she had decided to use as the schoolroom. They found that it was Mark's bedroom, which was very convenient, as Harriet whispered to him.

"Don't whisper, Harriet dear," said Miss Allison, who had her back turned, "it's unpardonably rude." She was doing something which looked like writing on an invisible blackboard. "There, that's finished. Now, Harriet, will you bring your back-board out of that corner and lie on it. I wish to see you on it for at least half an hour every day, to give you a ladylike and erect deportment."

Harriet had a look in the corner but saw nothing except Mark's tennis racket and a box of balls.

"I don't see it," she said unhappily.

"Nonsense, dear. Your left foot is on it at the moment. Try to be observant."

As Harriet's left foot was resting firmly on the floor, she felt rather injured, but, catching the governess' eye, she hastily stooped, picked up an imaginary back-board with both hands, and carried it to the middle of the room.

"It would help," she said to herself, "if I knew what the

dratted thing looked like. But I suppose it's as long as I am."

"Put it down, child. Now lie on it. Flat on your back, arms at your sides, eyes looking at the ceiling."

Harriet lay down on the floor, looking at Miss Allison doubtfully, and was rewarded by a nod.

"Now Mark," said the governess briskly, "I have written on the blackboard a list of Latin prepositions followed by the ablative case. You will occupy yourself in learning them while I write out an exercise for you both. Harriet, you can be trying to think of twenty wildflowers beginning with the letter *l*."

She sat down at an invisible table and began briskly writing on nothing. Mark looked gloomily at the empty space where the blackboard was supposed to be, and wondered how he could learn a list of words he couldn't see. This adventure, it seemed to him, was a bit too much like real life. He wished Miss Allison was a more conventional ghost with clanking chains.

Harriet gave him a grin, and then, as Miss Allison looked particularly preoccupied, she whispered:

"A, ab, absque, coram, de . . ."

Mark's face cleared. Of course, now he remembered the words. Thank goodness he had learned them at school. He thought for a moment anxiously of what would happen when they didn't know what she had written on the blackboard, but anyway, that was in the future. No use worrying about it now.

At the end of what was presumably half an hour, Miss Allison turned round.

"Well!" she said. "Harriet, you may put away your board. Mark, let me hear you recite. You should have it by rote now."

"A, ab, absque," he began.

"Never let me see you recite like that, Mark. Hands be-hind your back, feet in the first position, head up." Mark obeyed peevishly.

"Now begin again."

> "A, ab, absque, coram, de,
> Palam, clam, cum, ex and e
> Tenus, sine, pro, in, prae
> Ablative with these we spy."

"Very good Mark, though your pronunciation is a little modern," she said. "You may open that blue tin and have a caraway biscuit."

Mark looked about for a blue tin, saw none, and opened an imaginary one.

Harriet did rather badly over her wildflowers beginning with *l*. Half the ones she thought of, such as lady's smock, lady's slipper, lady's tresses, lords and ladies, and all the lesser stitchworts and lesser chickweeds were disqualified, leaving her with a very poor list. She got no caraway biscuit. However, as Mark's had been imaginary, she did not greatly mind.

After this, they had to do embroidery. It also was totally imaginary. They held invisible pieces of linen, threaded in-visible needles, and sometimes for the fun of the thing stuck them into their fingers and squeaked with imaginary pain. It was all very amusing. It soon appeared that even if they couldn't see their work, Miss Allison could. She kept up a running fire of comment, from which they gathered that Mark's was bad and Harriet's fairly good. This seemed rea-sonable enough. Mark was rather indignant at being expected to do embroidery, but after a while the governess began to read aloud to them a fascinating book called *Improving Tales*, all about some good children and some bad ones, so he just stuck his needle in and out and listened.

"There," said Miss Allison finally, "that will do for today. For your preparation you will both turn to page two hundred in your Latin grammars and learn the list of words beginning:

> Amnis, axis, caulis, collis,
> Clunis, crinis, fascis, follis—

and you will also each write me a composition entitled 'Devotion to Duty'."

"Please," said Harriet, "which is our Latin grammar?"

"Why, Crosby, of course. The blue book. Now run along, dears. You will want to get ready for your walk."

Mark wanted to go to bed, but she gave him such an extremely firm look that he went out with Harriet.

"You'll have to sleep on the sofa in my room," she whispered, "and creep back as soon as it's light. I wouldn't dare try to disobey her."

"Nor me," he whispered back. "She looks much firmer than any of the masters at school."

Luckily it was very warm, and there were some spare blankets in Harriet's room, so he was quite comfortable and slept well.

They were both rather silent and sleepy at breakfast, but afterwards on the river bank they discussed things.

"What are we going to do about those wretched essays?" asked Mark sourly. "I'm blowed if I write about devotion to duty."

"Oh, that's all right," Harriet replied. "Don't you see, the composition will be just like the embroidery. We'll show up an imaginary one."

"I don't quite understand that," said Mark, screwing up his

eyes and throwing stones into the mudbank; the tide was rapidly running out.

"Nor do I," agreed Harriet candidly, "but I *think* it's something like this: you see, she must have taught hundreds of children when she was alive, and I expect she made them all do embroidery and write about devotion to duty. So when we give her our imaginary things, she thinks about the ones she remembers. See what I mean?"

"Well, almost."

"No, what I'm worried about," Harriet went on, "is if she asks us to learn things and recite. Because if we haven't got the books to learn them from—like this wretched Crosby— we're stumped. Have you ever heard of Crosby?"

"No, we use Kennedy in our class."

"So do we. Well, maybe we could ask to write them down from memory instead of reciting them. It'll be all right, of course, if she asks us to learn something like *The Ancient Mariner*."

"I dunno," said Mark, "all this sounds a bit too much like work to me."

"It is a bit. Still, not many people have learned Latin prepositions from a ghost. That's something."

"I tell you," said Mark. "The attic."

"What about it?"

"There are hundreds of old boxes there with things in them that belong to the house. I was up there one day looking for secret passages. Maybe if we looked in them we'd find some old lesson books that belonged to the people who were here before."

"That's an idea. We might find something about Miss Allison too—a diary or something. Let's go now."

"Anyway," Harriet pointed out as they walked back to the

house, "if it does get too much of a good thing, we can always just stay in bed at night and not go to her."

"All right for you," said Mark, "but I expect she's in my room all the time. She'll probably just haul me out of bed at ten o'clock."

The lunch bell rang as they came up the garden, so they had to put off their search in the attic.

It was a dark, cool room, lit only by green glass tiles in the roof. Harriet sat for a while pensively on a box while Mark rummaged about, turning out with everything little piles of thickish yellow powder smelling of pine needles.

"That's for the moths," she said. Then she began folding the things and putting them back as he went on. They were mostly clothes folded in tissue paper, and old rush baskets pressed flat, large women's hats with draggled bunches of feathers, and pairs of kid gloves.

"People wore things like these in the 1914 war," said Harriet. "Look, here's a newspaper. January, 1919. This is too modern."

"Half a sec," said Mark, "over here they seem to be older." He pulled out an enormous flounced ball-dress of fawn-colored satin; some shawls; a pair of satin slippers; a little woven basket with a lid containing brightly colored glass bracelets and necklaces of glass beads; a large flat box full of fans— ivory, with pink flowers, satinwood, and wonderful plumy feathers.

"I wish there were some letters or books or something," Mark murmured discontentedly. Harriet was exclaiming to herself over the fans before laying them back in the box.

"This one's very heavy," said Mark, tugging at a chest. The

lid came up unwillingly. Underneath was a gorgeous Chinese hanging of stiff silk, folded square. He lifted it out.

"Aha!" A heavy, old fashioned Bible lay on the tissue paper.

"Harriet, look here!"

Harriet came across and read over her brother's shoulder the inscription in a beautiful copperplate handwriting: "To my dear daughter Georgiana Lucy Allison from her affectionate Mother, Christmas 1831."

"Well!" they breathed at each other. Mark flipped through the leaves, but there was nothing else, except for a faded pansy.

"Let's see what else there is in the box."

Underneath the tissue paper were more books.

"Lesson books," said Harriet ecstatically. "*Primer of Geography. Mason's Manual of Arithmetic.* Look! Here's Crosby's *Latin Grammar Made Easy.*"

Besides the lesson books there were children's books—*Improving Tales for the Young, Tales for Little Folks, Good Deeds in a Bad World, Tales from the Gospel,* and a number of others, all improving. Several of them also had Miss Allison's name in them. Others had children's names—"John, from his affec. Governess," "Lucy, from Mamma," and in a large stumbling script "Lucy, from Isabel."

"We'd better take down all the lesson books," said Harriet. "They can live on the bookshelf in your room—there's plenty of empty space."

They had a further search in the other boxes, but found nothing else interesting except some children's clothes—sailor suits, dresses and pantalets, which Harriet would have liked to try on. "But they look so fragile," she said with a sigh, "I'd probably tear them." So everything was replaced, and they went downstairs, each with an armful of books.

Later that evening Harriet's mother found her sprawled on the drawing-room sofa looking at a book and then shutting it and muttering to herself.

"You look as if you were learning poetry," said Mrs. Armitage, glancing over her shoulder. "What, *Latin!* Good heavens, I have got diligent children. Incidentally I wish you'd find another tune to practice on the piano. I find myself singing that *'Lieber Augustin'* all day long."

That night, when Harriet went along to Mark's room at about midnight, she found him already hard at work reciting the principal parts of Latin verbs.

"Mark knows his list of words very well, Harriet. I trust that you will also be able to earn your caraway biscuit," remarked Miss Allison and then, while Harriet lay on her imaginary back-board, the governess read them a long, boring chapter about the Wars of the Roses.

"I generally start my pupils at the *beginning* of history, with William the Conqueror," explained Miss Allison, "but your dear Mother expressed a wish for you to study this period particularly."

Afterwards Harriet recited her Latin and also earned a caraway biscuit. Then Harriet and Mark showed her their invisible essays on Duty, and Harriet's point was proved. Miss Allison obviously saw them, even if the children didn't, and peevishly pointed out several spelling mistakes.

"Mark, you will write out the word 'ceiling' fifty times," she said. "That will be all for this morning, dears. Harriet, will you ask Anne to run up with a duster, and I will dust my room myself. And tell her that she forgot to sweep under the bed yesterday, though I reminded her particularly."

"Mother," said Mark one morning. "Can I change my bedroom? I'd much rather sleep in the room next to Harriet."

"Well, if you do," said his mother, looking at him acutely, "you must promise not to be popping in and out of each other's rooms all night. I thought I heard something last night." But they gazed at her so innocently that she agreed and said they could change the things over themselves.

"Just as well," said Mark, when they were carrying sheets along the passage. "Do you know she hauled me out of bed last night and asked me what I thought I was doing sleeping on the schoolroom sofa."

"She *is* queer," Harriet remarked thoughtfully, "I sometimes wonder if she really *sees* us at all. She obviously doesn't see the same furniture as we do, because sometimes she uses tables and chairs that aren't there, and when she talks about our parents, she doesn't mean Mother and Father, because they never said anything to her about the Wars of the Roses."

"And there's all this business about Anne and Cook, too. I suppose she sort of sees them all round. Poor old thing," said Mark, tucking in a lump of blanket, "I'm getting quite fond of her."

"You know, I'm sure she has something on her mind,"

added Harriet. "She looks so worried at times, as if she was trying to remember things."

It soon appeared that the children had something on their minds, too.

"You both of you look dreadfully tired nowadays," remarked Mrs. Armitage. "You aren't sickening for measles, are you? And don't you think you're overdoing this holiday work a bit? Surely you don't need to do all that Latin and History. The other afternoon when you were asleep on the lawn, Mark, I heard you muttering the dates of the kings of England in your sleep. Take a bit of rest from it. By the way, there's an Admiral Lecacheur coming to tea this afternoon—he lives in that little house on the river you've taken such a fancy to. If you want to get invited to have a look round it, you'd better put in an appearance."

"Lecacheur?" said Mark vaguely, "I seem to know the name."

"Yes, it's the family who lived here before. He's the owner of this house, actually, but he's mostly away, so he prefers to let it and live in the cottage."

Lecacheur! Of course it was the name written in the lesson books! Mark and Harriet exchanged a swift, excited look.

"Is he an old man?" asked Mark carelessly.

"About sixty, I believe. Now I must fly, I've masses to do. Be good, children."

"If he's about sixty," said Harriet, when they were alone, "he must have been born in 1885. I *wish* we knew when Miss Allison died."

"Well, we know she was alive in 1831 because of the Bible. I wonder how old she was when she was given that?"

"Say she was about ten," said Harriet, counting on her

fingers, "that makes her sixty-five when the Admiral was born. Well, that's quite possible. She looks more than that. He may easily have known her. We'll have to draw him out, somehow."

"Maybe, if he knew her, he'd know what it is she worries about," said Harriet hopefully. "You know, I believe if we could find out what's on her mind and help her, she'd vanish. That's the sort of thing ghosts do."

"Well, I'm not sure I'd be sorry," said Mark, puffing out a deep breath. "I'd like a night's sleep for once. Remember when we didn't wake up, how cross she was next night? And I've had just about enough Latin verbs. *And* the kings of England."

Harriet agreed. "And the parents are beginning to think that there's something funny going on. Father started whistling '*Lieber Augustin*' the other day, and then he turned and gave me an *awfully* queer look."

Admiral Lecacheur turned out to be a pleasant man, large, jovial, gray-haired. It was not difficult for the children to get an invitation from him to go and look at his cottage.

As he showed them the stuffed shark and the model ships in bottles, Harriet summoned up the courage to speak.

"Admiral," she finally said timidly, "did you ever know a Miss Georgiana Lucy Allison?"

"God bless my soul, yes," he said, turning round and smiling at her. "She was our family governess. Is there some stuff of hers still knocking about the house?"

"Yes, there are some books of hers. And a Bible."

"Old Allie," he said reminiscently. "She was a wonderful old girl. Must have been with our family for fifty years. She taught three generations of us. I was the last."

"Did she teach you?"

"I remember her very well," he went on, without noticing the interruption, "though she died, I suppose, when I was about five. That would be around eighteen-ninety. But she'd already taught me to read, and some of the multiplication table, and the kings of England. She was great on learning things by heart. Not like the modern education you get now, I daresay. 'Cedric,' she used to say, 'how will you ever get on in life if you don't know these things?' Ah, well. Here I am an admiral, and I daresay if she'd taught me longer, I should have been Admiral of the Fleet. But there! She must have died more than fifty years ago."

He smiled at their serious faces and said, "Now here's a thing you ought to like. Just look at the size of that!" And he handed Harriet a shell the size of a dinner plate.

"Well, we still don't know what's on her mind," said Mark, as they walked homewards.

"No, but we couldn't ask him all at once. Another time we'll jolly well pump him."

But as things turned out they didn't need to. That night when Mark was reciting the dates of the kings of England, he absentmindedly followed William and Mary with "Queen Anne, 1700."

There was an ominous pause, and Miss Allison suddenly burst into tears.

"Cedric, you wicked boy," she sobbed, "will you *never* get it right? How can you expect to be a success in life, if you don't know your dates? And you going into the Navy, too." She hid her face in her hands, but through them they could hear her say, "I'm getting so old. How can I die happy if that boy doesn't know the date of Queen Anne? All the others learned it."

"Please don't cry," said Mark awkwardly, patting her

shoulder. "It was only a mistake. I do know it. Really I do. It's 1702, isn't it?"

But she went on sobbing "Cedric! Cedric!" and after a minute Harriet touched his arm and pulled him softly out of the room.

"Let's go to bed," she whispered. "We can't do anything about her. And I've got a brilliant idea. Tell you in the morning."

Next day she dragged him down to Dolphin Cottage. The Admiral was surprised to see them. "What, you again so early? You're just in time to help me syringe my greenfly."

"Admiral," said Harriet, fixing her eyes on him earnestly, "will you tell me something terribly important?"

"What is it," he said, very much astonished.

"Tell me when Queen Anne came to the throne."

He burst into a great roar of laughter, slapping his knees. "Well, I'm blessed; do you know, it's funny you should ask me that, because it's the one date I never have been able to remember. Miss Allison used to get wild about it. 'I shan't die happy till you know that date, Cedric,' she used to say. But she did die, poor old soul, and I don't know it to this day."

"Come and sit down," said Harriet, dragging him to a garden seat. One on each side, she and Mark told him the whole story. When he heard how Miss Allison made their nights a burden, he shouted with laughter.

"That's just like her, bless her," he exclaimed.

"So you see, it really has got to stop," Harriet explained. "We're getting worn out, and I'm sure she is too—after all she must be about a hundred and twenty, far too old to be teaching. And she's so miserable, poor dear. I think you can help us."

She told him their plan, and after some hesitation the

Admiral agreed. "But if you're pulling my leg," he threatened, "you'll never forget it, the pair of you."

"Now you've got to learn it," said Harriet. "Write it on a bit of paper somewhere—here, I'll do it for you. Now stick it up where you'll be able to see it all day. And we'll meet you at the garden gate tonight at midnight."

"What your parents would say if they caught us—" he exclaimed, but he agreed. The children went home very hopeful.

The meeting came off as arranged. They let him in by the garden door and took him quietly up the back stairs into the schoolroom, where Miss Allison was pacing up and down looking very impatient.

"What time," she began, and then suddenly she saw who was with them. "Why, *Cedric!*"

"Allie!" he exclaimed.

"You wicked boy! Where have you been all this time?"

"I'm sorry," he said meekly, looking more like a small boy than a gray-haired man of sixty.

"Just you tell me one thing," she said, drawing herself up and giving him a piercing look. "When did Queen Anne come to the throne?"

The children gazed at him anxiously, but they need not have worried. He had learned his lesson this time.

"Seventeen-two," he said promptly, and they sighed with relief.

Miss Allison burst into tears of joy.

"I might have known it," she sobbed. "My good boy. Why, now you know that, you might even become an admiral, and I can die happy."

And as they watched her, suddenly, flick! like a candle, she went out, and there was no one in the room but their three selves.

"Well, I'm blessed," said the Admiral, not for the first time. "Old Allie." He walked quietly from the room. Mark saw him down to the garden gate. When he came back, he found Harriet dabbing at her eyes with a handkerchief.

"You know, I'm going to miss her," she said. "Oh, well, let's go to bed."

They never saw Miss Allison again.

The Land of Trees and Heroes

The children had had whooping cough, rather badly, and although they were now well past the distressing stage of going black in the face, crowing, and having to rush from the room, they were still thin, pale, and cross. Mrs. Armitage decided that they had better lose a bit more schooling and go to stay with Grandmother for a change of air. Mark and Harriet received the news listlessly. There seemed to be so many snags and prohibitions about going to Grandmother's.

"You'll have to wear rubber-soled shoes all the time."

"Why, can't Granny stand noise?" asked Harriet.

"No, it's not that, but the floors are so highly polished; well I remember the time your father broke his leg coming downstairs. And of course you must amuse yourselves and not bother Grandmother. She hasn't much time for children."

"Wouldn't it be better if we stayed at home?" Mark's tone was glum.

"No; a change is what you need. And we shall all be so busy here, with this wretched by-election." Mark's mother's tone showed slight relief, indeed, at the thought that her children would be out of the way at this time; they had been known to upset local arrangements.

Grandmother's house was huge, old, and dark; Mark and Harriet tiptoed about in it like two white mice in a cave. Not that Grandmother was unkind; in her vague way she seemed pleased to see them. But after they had been staying with her a day or two, Mark and Harriet understood better what their mother had meant when she said that Granny hadn't much time for children. The old lady was not exactly busy, but most of the time her attention was very much elsewhere.

"Put away that bayonet, Roger," she would say absently, "how many times do I have to tell you that it will rust if you don't give it a rub when you bring it into the tent. And hang up your balaclava and ask that Sepoy what he thinks he is doing."

For Granny was very, very old, and had traveled with Grandfather (dead long ago) all over the world, and seen many battles, from Inkermann to Mafeking. She was also extremely deaf and seemed to understand only about a tenth of what the children said to her as she sat knitting, placid and withdrawn, by the log fire that always burned in the great hearth. They got most of their advice and information from Nursie, who was almost as old as Grandmother, but was not deaf and took an active interest in their goings-on.

"Why is there a telephone in the orchard?" Harriet wanted to know.

"Ah, there, Miss Harriet, dear. Always asking questions like your father before you. Why should it be there but in case your Granny wanted to ring up the orchard, then?"

"But there's nobody to answer—only a lot of apple trees."

"And if you're going to speak to an apple tree, better ring up than walk all that way on foot at her age," said Nursie, which only muddled Harriet more and didn't explain matters in the least. She went on thinking that it was very odd indeed to see a telephone all by itself among the trees, standing on a little pedestal in the grass, with a dovecot roof over it to keep the rain off.

"And why does Granny keep all those musical things hanging in the trees if she can't hear them?" asked Mark.

"Ee-yolian harps those are, Master Mark, and the others is wind-bells. And as to why she keeps them there—well, there's sounds as the ear can't hear, isn't there? Bats' squeaks, and that?"

"Yes," said Mark doubtfully.

"Well, then, maybe Granny can hear those! Now run along, the pair of you, and don't bother me. Play anywhere in the garden, climb any of the trees, but don't break any branches. And don't go climbing the laurel tree or the Silver Lady will get you."

"Oh, who is the Silver Lady? Tell? Do tell!"

"The Silver Lady? Why, she owns the laurel tree, of course. Climb into her tree and she'll send you to sleep. There's a rhyme about it:

Sleep in the laurel but for an hour
You'll sleep in the Silver Lady's power.

So mind you keep out of it—nasty dangerous thing."

The children wanted to hear more about the Silver Lady, but Nursie pushed them crossly out, muttering that Silver Lady or no Silver Lady, she'd got to get her silver polished by lunch time, and they wandered into the garden, shivering and forlorn, telling each other that it wasn't worth starting any game before lunch.

Many of the trees were hung with these strange aeolian harps, or with the silvery glass bells, and it must have been a sheltered part of the country thereabouts, for only very occasionally, when some wandering gust found its way through the trees, did there come a twangling and a sighing from high among the branches. Lying awake and coughing at night, Mark often hoped for a snatch of wind-music to breathe him off to sleep, but, perhaps owing to the immense thickness of the solid old walls, it was seldom that a far-off note whispered against his ear.

At five o'clock every evening Granny took off her hearing aid and settled down in front of the television; at the same time Nursie removed her thick glasses, without which she could not see more than a couple of yards, and dragged her favorite upright chair close beside the radio, turned on loud; from that minute on, the two old women were quite lost to the children, who would find their supper of bread-and-milk and beef tea (or bread-and-dripping and cocoa) set out on the kitchen table. The kitchen was one of the nicest rooms of the house: huge, but airy and warm, with a great open range, and here they would eat, read, talk, play a leisurely game of ludo and take themselves off to bed.

The nights were bad.

They slept next door to each other, and if Mark managed to get off to sleep for half an hour, Harriet was sure to have a shattering burst of coughing and wake him up. Then she would doze off until Mark waked her in his turn. They felt that their coughing shook the house from end to end, but of course Granny never heard them at all, and it took ages before Nursie would come muttering and tutting along in her red flanel dressing gown and give them hot drinks of lemon barley. And sometimes, on account of her short sightedness and not putting on her glasses in the night-time, she would rub their chests with the lemon barley (very sticky) and give them hot camphorated oil to drink. Still, it was nice to have her exclaiming round them like a cross old ghost, and sometimes she sang them to sleep with old, old nursery rhymes—

> "Intery mintery, cuttery corn,
> Apple seed and apple thorn . . ."

in her quavering, wavering voice which seemed to search all round the corners of the room before finding its note.

"Now, that's enough: you must go to sleep," she would finally say severely, and at this point the children (Harriet would have come in by now and would be sitting, wrapped in eider downs, on Mark's bed) always pleaded:

"Oh, please, *The Land of Trees and Heroes* before you go, please!"

And Nursie would sing:

> "In the land of trees and heroes
> The tawny owl is king
> Who locked the door, who holds the key
> Hidden beneath his wing."

"Tell us some more about the land, Nursie?"

"That's all there is, and it's time you went to sleep anyway." They never got more than the one verse out of her, which ended on a plaintive, unfinished note, but there was something about the song that made them long to know more. Where was the land? And who the heroes? And why was the key hidden? Nursie wouldn't say.

The children still felt too tired and convalescent to play strenuous games, or go riding, or take long walks; they spent most of their outdoor time slowly and haphazardly exploring Granny's enormous neglected garden.

One cold, nasty afternoon, rummaging in the summer house at the end of the lawn, they found an old bow with a leather cover and a red velvet guard. There was a target, too, but no arrows.

Mark dragged the target, molting straw at the seams, out onto the lawn, and said, "We can easily make some arrows. Never mind about feathers. Hazel's the best wood."

"Nursie said not to break any branches," Harriet reminded him doubtfully, but she rubbed her finger up and down the smooth springiness of the bow; it did seem a pity not to use it.

"Oh, she only meant big ones I expect."

They couldn't find any hazels, but there was an elder bush growing by the summer house with a lot of straight young branches shooting in the thick of it; Mark took out his pen-knife and cut three of these, while Harriet, to be on the safe side, politely asked the elder tree if she minded their taking this liberty. There was no reply; she had hardly expected there would be.

"They're rather light but they'll do for a start, to practice with," Mark said.

He whittled off the leaves and twigs, and cut a bowstring

notch in each wand, while Harriet stood hugging her arms together, watching him.

"Now then, watch!"

Stringing the bow, he carefully fitted one of his arrows and fired, aiming high. The light, pithy arrow soared high and began a beautiful curve towards the target, but at that moment a gentle wind sprang up and turned it sideways so that it swerved and landed in the laurel tree.

"Oh, blow!" said Mark. "That's the first wind there's been this afternoon. Hark at the wind-bells! It would happen just when I fired."

He ran towards the tree.

"Wait!" shouted Harriet, dashing after him. "What are you doing?"

"Going to get the arrow!"

"But don't you remember—the Silver Lady!"

"Oh, blow it—I'm not going to stay in the tree an hour! It won't take two twos to nip up and get the arrow down. I can see it from here."

"Do be careful—" She arrived at the tree just as he swung himself into the first crotch and stood with her hands on the trunk, anxiously looking up after him.

"I can almost reach it now," he called in a moment, from somewhere up in the thickness of the tree. "Goodness, there's a cat up here—it seems to be fast asleep! And a whole lot of birds, asleep too. How peculiar."

"Oh, do hurry up!"

"And here's a satchel." Mark's voice was muffled now by the thick green leaves among which he was scuffling and flapping. "Good lord, I say, there's a postman asleep up here—I never saw him climb up, did you? And there's something that looks like a butcher's basket full of chops. This is the oddest tree I've ever been . . ." His voice trailed away on a tremendous yawn.

"Mark!" shouted Harriet, her voice sharp with anxiety.

No answer.

"Mark!" Twisting her head, she peered up, looking into the dark cave. And then she saw Mark. He was fourteen or fifteen feet up, curled as comfortably into a fork of the tree as if he were lying in a hammock, and he was fast asleep, his head pillowed on his hand. In the fork below him was a big tabby cat, also fast asleep, and over to the left she could dimly make out a butcher's boy in a striped blue-and-white apron, sleeping wedged in a nest of crisscrossing branches.

Harriet shouted till she was hoarse, and shook the tree till she started herself coughing, but there was no reply from any of the peaceful sleepers.

"Oh, goodness," she said to herself miserably, "I knew something like this would happen. Now what had I better do?"

Telling Nursie seemed the first step, and Harriet went indoors. But five o'clock had struck and Nursie was listening to a program of young artists from the Midlands, and was not to be disturbed. She waved Harriet away with a preoccupied hand.

"If I don't get Mark out of that tree before the hour's up," Harriet thought, "we shall never be able to wake him. I wonder if I could drag him out by myself?"

She went back to the tree but decided that it would be too risky, even if she put a ladder against Mark's fork and climbed up it; Mark was much too heavy for her to lift, and if he fell from that height, he might easily break something. Besides, something ought to be done about the postman and the butcher's boy too; goodness knows how long they had been there.

"I know," she thought. "I'll go for the doctor."

Dr. Groves had the house at the end of the village nearest Granny's. They had been to see him when they first arrived, for a check-over, and had liked him very much.

"He'll be able to help," Harriet thought.

She ran round to the shed by the stables and got out Nursie's bicycle; this was no time for loitering. Nursie would not be wanting it again before morning anyway, and, without waiting to ask permission, Harriet sped off down the front path and took the steps at a slither.

Thank goodness it was not a surgery night, and Dr. Groves was sitting by his fire, peacefully reading the *Lancet*, when Harriet arrived, panting and gasping, about five minutes later.

"Please will you help me," she wheezed, trying not to cough. "Mark's gone to sleep in the laurel tree."

"Eh, dear, has he now," said Dr. Groves. "And you want me to help pull him down, is that it?"

"Yes, please. And there are two other people up in the tree, and a cat; I expect they ought to come down too."

"Tut, tut." The doctor sounded more disapproving than surprised. "And what would they have been doing up there, I wonder?"

"I don't know. One of them's the postman. Oh, do please hurry."

"I can't hurry much, my lass, on account of my leg. Eh, well, well, now, the postman. We'd been wondering where he'd got to when he vanished last May."

He pulled himself stiffly to his feet, and Harriet remembered with dismay that he had an artificial leg.

"Should I get somebody else?" she said anxiously. "Will it be too much for you?"

"No, no, I'll manage very well. Just pass me that stick, will you now, and I'll be with you directly."

They made slow progress back up the road, and Harriet did rings around the doctor in her impatience to get on.

"Ah, it's a great convenience to me, this leg," he said imperturbably, as he clanked along. "Bitten off by a shark, it was, in the days when I was a bold buccaneering sea-doctor, and I fitted myself up with the best cast-iron peg I could lay hands on. I can use it for poking the fire or bowling over a charging tiger—and best of all, when some fussing woman gets a pain in her little finger and fancies sending for the doctor, she thinks again and says to herself: 'With his iron leg it'll take him an hour and twenty minutes to get here; it's not worth fetching him out,' and that saves me a great, great deal of trouble, I can tell you, for I'm a lazy old man and never do two trips where one will do."

"Oh, yes, I'm sure it does," said Harriet, wheeling round him distractedly. "Are you sure you wouldn't like to ride Nursie's bicycle?"

"No, thank you, my bairn, riding a bicycle's one of the things I can *not* do with this leg. But we're managing very well, very well indeed."

Dusk was falling as he stumped up Granny's steps, and Harriet looked at her watch and saw with a sinking heart that it had taken them forty-five minutes to do the return journey; Mark must have been in the laurel tree for very nearly an hour.

"Ah, yes, there they are," Dr. Groves said, pulling a flashlight from his pocket and shining it up into the tree. "Fast asleep, the three of them. And Pussie Baudrons too, after birds, nae doubt, the naughty grimalkin. And that's an interesting thing, very interesting indeed, that the laurel tree should have such power. When I was a boy I would always use laurel leaves for putting butterflies to sleep. In a jam jar."

Without listening to his reflections, which seemed likely to go on for ever, Harriet dashed off and came back with Granny's aluminum fruit-picking ladder, which she planted firmly against the trunk of the laurel.

Dr. Groves had embarked on a learned chat with himself about the medical properties of various plants, so she started up the ladder, saying over her shoulder:

"If I pull them down, Dr. Groves, do you think you can catch them?"

"I'll do my best, lass. Feet first is the way, feet first, now. Don't let the poor slumberers fall on their heads or you'd do better to leave them bide where they are."

The butcher's boy was the nearest, and Harriet tugged him down cautiously, being most careful herself not to get into the tree even for a moment. Dr. Groves received the long dangling legs and flopped the boy onto the ground, where he lay limp and sprawling. Harriet dropped his basket of chops (they flew in all directions), had to come down, then, and move her ladder round to the other side in order to reach Mark, who was more of a problem; half lifting, half dragging, she at last managed to get him clear of the branches and lower him to the doctor. He was laid down unceremoniously on the chops while they tackled the postman. He was the most difficult of all, for he was higher up still, and in the end Harriet had to go and get the clothesline and make a very unworkmanlike hitch round his shoulders so that she could let him bumpingly down to the doctor. She herself had to come down from time to time to get a good breath of fresh air, for even when she was safely perched on the ladder she found that the laurel tree made her feel uncommonly sleepy.

"And here's the cat but I'm not going to risk being caught by the Silver Lady for a lot of starlings," she said descending for the last time with the tabby slumped peacefully under her arm. "What shall we do with them now?"

"Eh, well, there's little can be done till I've reflected," said the doctor, who seemed to be infected by the general somnolence, and was yawning dreadfully. "We'll just get them indoors safe and snug and then I'll be off home. I'll come up in the morning for a confabulation with your Granny. Meanwhile they'll take no harm."

Using the barrow for the longer stretch of the journey, they carted the slumberers into a sort of garden room, where they were propped about in canvas swings and deck chairs, and covered with tartan rugs. The rising moon silvered the three inert bundles (and one small one) through the window. Harriet and the doctor stepped out, closing the glass door behind them, and the doctor's peg-legged shadow stretched out, long and fantastic, across the lawn, as he stumped off with a good-night wave.

Harriet turned indoors, feeling rather forlorn. She didn't want any supper, and went straight upstairs to bed. The whole house was as quiet as a stringless harp, and she missed Mark's companionable coughing from next door. Nevertheless, she managed to fall asleep in fifteen minutes or so and drifted into some very strange dreams about flying cats, laurel trees full of sharks and a Silver Lady with a wooden leg. "You give me back my brother!" shouted Harriet, and at once became aware that she was coughing, and that she was awake.

"Eh, nonny, nonny, what's all this?" said Nursie, materializing beside the bed with her candle and red dressing gown. "Here you are then, my duck, here's a drink of black currant for that cough." Harriet obediently swallowed it down. It tasted like permanganate.

"Nursie," she said miserably, "we've lost Mark. The Silver Lady's got him—he's asleep and won't wake up."

"Laws-a-me," said Nursie sharply, "he's been up the laurel tree then? All the same they are—tell them not to do a thing and they run straight away and do it. A good sleep'll work wonders for his cough, that's one comfort."

"But how are we going to wake him? The postman's been asleep since May."

"As to that," Nursie answered, "I couldn't say. The rhyme says:

> Those by the silver slumber taken
> Only the Tawny Owl can waken.

But I can hear a couple of owls down in the orchard this minute and it takes more than them to waken Master Mark in the normal way, let alone when the Silver Lady's put her finger on him. We'll think about it in the morning, Miss Harriet dear. Deary me, there's the telephone ringing at half past nine at night, of all the ungodly times."

And blowing out her candle she tiptoed away.

The telephone was the children's father ringing up to ask if they were behaving themselves. Nursie told him to hold on while she went and fetched Granny from the television, explaining to her on the way what had happened to Mark.

"That you, Mother? How are you?" shouted Mr. Armitage, loud enough to penetrate Granny's deafness.

"I am well, thank you, Geoffrey. The children are looking much better."

"Behaving all right?"

"There is no need to shout, Geoffrey, I can hear perfectly

well over the telephone. Mark is unfortunately in a coma; all the fault of the Silver Lady, you know. Otherwise nothing out of the common has occurred."

"What? what?" shouted Mr. Armitage, becoming very agitated. "What are you doing about it?"

"Why, my dear boy, there is nothing to be done. It is my bedtime now, good night." And Granny firmly rang off, leaving Mr. Armitage in a great state of irritation.

The dying tink of the telephone came to Harriet as she lay wide awake and worrying in a patch of moonlight. Something ought to be done about Mark soon, she was sure; otherwise he might sink so deep into sleep that he could *never* be awakened. And then all their plans for Christmas would be spoiled. Not to mention camping out during the Easter holidays.

The Tawny Owl, Nursie had said. There was a tawny owl, too, in the rhyme about the land of trees and heroes. Perhaps it was the same one? In any case, the time to find a tawny owl was now, while it was dark and the owls were abroad, not tomorrow morning when they were all fast asleep and hidden away in thickets.

Harriet had by now thought herself wide awake, and she got up silently and began putting on her clothes again. The sound of the telephone had given her an idea. It seemed so wild and odd that she hardly liked to put it to herself in actual thought, but she slipped out of her room, carrying her shoes in her hand, and went downstairs to the little telephone room off the front hall. The house was silent again. Nursie and Granny had gone to bed. Only the faint crackle of coal settling for the night came from the kitchen stove.

Harriet sat looking at the telephone in its little pool of moonlight. How did you ring up an orchard? In the end she dialed "O".

For a long, long time she could hear ringing, but nobody answered. She almost gave up in despair and put the receiver back, but then she thought she might as well wait a bit longer. At last the ringing stopped, there came a click, and she could hear a far-off sighing, like the wind in the branches.

"Who is there?" she asked, rather nervously.

A whisper answered her. "Cox's Ooooor-ange Pippin speeee-king . . ." it murmured leafily against her ear. "To whoooooom did you wissssssh to speeeeeeeek?"

"May I please speak to the Tawny Owl?" Harriet's heart beat in triumph at this success.

"Hold on, pleasssssss . . ." whispered Cox's Orange, and there was another long pause, a long, long pause, while Harriet heard, down the receiver, the trees in the orchard all turning their branches this way and that against the night sky.

Presently there came a click as if somebody had picked up the receiver.

"I—is that the Tawny Owl?" Harriet asked nervously.

"Who?"

"I asked to speak to the Tawny Owl."

"To who?"

"You mean to whom," Harriet was on the point of saying, when she realized that it *was* the Tawny Owl speaking. She explained the trouble they were in, and that he was their only hope. "Oh, please, Sir," she ended despairingly, "won't you help us? I'm sure Dr. Groves won't have much idea what to do."

"You will need ammunition," said the Tawny Owl. "To wit, a bow and some arrows."

"I can manage that." Harriet was much encouraged by his

voice—a friendly, brown, furry sort of voice. "What shall I do with them?"

"Bring them to the laurel tree. Do not delay. I will be there."

"Oh, *thank* you," Harriet said gratefully.

"Who?"

"You—oh, I mean whooo," she replied politely, put the receiver back and ran tiptoeing into the garden room, where she had left the bow and the remaining two arrows. Everyone was breathing peacefully, and she went out, making snail tracks in the moony dew, across the lawn to the laurel tree.

She had not been there a moment when the branches parted and a large pale shape coasted silently down and landed as lightly as a dead leaf on her shoulder. She felt the smoothness of feathers against her cheek.

"Whooo," the Tawny Owl said gently in her ear. "The arrows—of what wood are they?"

"Elder."

"A moody personality. Was permission obtained? It would not do to be rude to her."

"We—we *asked*," said Harriet anxiously, "but she didn't answer."

"I will inquire anew. Do you procure a bicycle and return hither—be swift. Adieu."

Quick as she was, the owl had returned to the tree before her.

"Elder is graciously pleased to allow the use of those two. It is a propitious wood. Now! We must go fast. I will sit on your shoulder and instruct you as to the route," said the Tawny Owl.

He soon found, however, that it was easier if he flew ahead and Harriet followed, for he could go much faster. Whizzing

after him down the garden path, Harriet realized that she was not going to have time to dismount for the steps and discovered, without much surprise, halfway down them that she had become air-borne and was pedaling briskly after the owl ten feet above the white surface of the road, which streamed away like a nylon ribbon beneath her.

"Where are we going?" she called after him.

"To the land," his hoot came faintly back between wing-beats, "to the land of trees and heroes . . ."

It was a wonderful ride. Harriet would not have minded going on all night, seeing the moon-silvered fields sliding under her feet and breathing the sharp cold scent of the trees when they swooped through the darkness of a wood. But presently she found that they were toiling up a long, cloudy ascent; the Tawny Owl went more slowly, and she herself was glad of Nursie's three-speed. Great cliffs of cloud built up on either side, drifts of loose cloud sometimes obscured the path, and at length they came to a door.

The owl flew up against it and clung, as a woodpecker or nuthatch will cling to the side of a tree, and in a moment or two the door swung open and they passed through.

Harriet often wished afterwards that she had had more time to notice the beauties of that land. It was smooth and rolling—a country like a counterpane of grassy downs and small groves on the hilltops, set with statues that shone white, here and there, against the trees. And strolling on the grass, or lying in the shade, some near, some far, were the heroes. Many of them she recognized at once. There was Hercules, doing his best, with the assistance of two grass snakes, to copy the position of a statue of himself, but the snakes were not being cooperative and he was not managing very well. There was Jason, with only one sandal. There were Prince Hal, gal-

loping about on a fiery horse, with Ivanhoe; Davy Crockett
and Robin Hood, having a shooting match; Captain Nemo
and Captain Ahab, having a nice chat in the shade. Harriet
saw with wonder, not unmixed with envy, that the postman
was sitting and chatting with them, a large tabby on his lap;
that the butcher's boy was playing bowls with Sir Francis
Drake and Sir Walter Raleigh; and that Bellerophon was giving Mark a ride on Pegasus.

"How did they get here?" she asked in astonishment.

"They are dreaming," the Tawny Owl answered her. She
had propped her bicycle against an ilex tree, and the owl was
once more sitting on her shoulder. "But now you must not
delay—the Silver Lady will soon be returning and you must
shoot her."

"I don't much want to shoot anybody," Harriet said doubtfully.

"She will take no harm from it. And only thus will you
have power over her, to make her let your brother free.
Watch, now—"

"String your bow," said Robin Hood, who had strolled up
and stood watching with friendly interest. "Then you'll be
ready. Like this."

Several other heroes gathered round with encouragement
and advice as Harriet strung her bow and pointed it at the
sky. Bellerophon grounded Pegasus in case of accidents.
"Isn't this a grand place?" Mark shouted to Harriet.

"There she goes!" suddenly came a cry from the watchers,
and Harriet saw something silvery and unbelievably swift
streak across the sky towards the moon.

"Quick!" the Tawny Owl murmured, "before she hides. Or
you will have to wait for twenty-four hours."

Harriet shot after the flashing figure.

"Oh!" came a long-drawn cry from the watchers. "You've shot the moon!"

And so indeed she had. Down it came, tumbling and drifting, like a great silver honesty pod falling through leaves of air. All the shadows rushed upward.

Harriet was appalled. But Ivanhoe, galloping up to where the moon lay blazing coldly (it was about the size of a nursery table), shouted, "You've caught her!"

"Make haste!" called Jason.

Harriet ran to the moon. It had fallen on its edge and was standing upright. The arrow, thrust clean through, was still quivering. And on the far side of the moon the Silver Lady struggled angrily to be free. The arrow had caught the bracelet on her wrist, and she was a prisoner, fastened by her hand to the shining disk. She was very beautiful, but her rage was frightening and Harriet hesitated before approaching her; the air all around her was bitterly cold, and Harriet felt as if she might freeze to the ground.

"Don't be afraid," said the Tawny Owl in her ear, and he called to the lady, "Mistress, the child has beaten you fairly."

"Not without your help and counsel," the Silver Lady replied, giving him a black look. "Well, child, what is it you want? Quick! Selene is not to be humiliated for long."

"I—I want you to set my brother free, please," Harriet said hurriedly. "And the postman and the butcher's boy and the cat."

"Is that all? You might have asked for kingdoms while you were about it." And the Silver Lady blew in the direction of Mark, who vanished like a pricked bubble. The postman and butcher's boy disappeared at the same time. Then, twisting her bracelet free from the arrow, the Silver Lady smiled at

Harriet enchantingly and shot upwards like a spark into the Milky Way.

"You must put back the moon," she called over her shoulder, "or you will be my next prisoner."

Put back the moon! Harriet stared at it in horror. How was that ever to be accomplished? But Perseus grinned at her reassuringly, tugged it out of the ground, and, leaning backwards, slung it up with a mighty swing of his arm.

Higher and higher the moon soared, and finally steadied, like a kite that feels the pull of the wind, and sailed among its accustomed stars.

"Homeward, now," the Tawny Owl warned Harriet. "Dawn approaches, when the road is closed."

It was a race home, through the mighty door, down the slopes of paling clouds. The stars were thinning out in the sky as Harriet and the owl covered the last furlong, and the bearings on Nursie's bicycle were red hot.

"Owl," said Harriet when they stood again below the laurel tree, "is the tree disenchanted now?"

"Oh, no," said the owl. "The tree is Selene's, and will always be hers. Just as the other trees in your grandmother's garden each belong to a different Power. Did you not know? The Elder, the Quince, and the dark-berried Yew . . ." His voice was trailing away as if he were yawning, and he murmured, "Adieu," gave Harriet's ear a little peck just as the sun rose, and flitted silently off to a lilac thicket.

Harriet watched him go with regret. There were so many things she had wanted to ask him.

"There!" Nursie clucked in triumph at breakfast, giving a saucerful of bacon rinds to the tabby cat. "Didn't I say a night's rest would finish the spell?"

"No," Harriet said, but she yawned as she said it, and the

clatter of knives and forks drowned her voice anyway. Mark, the postman, and the butcher's boy were eating an enormous breakfast. In the middle of it Doctor Groves stumped in and heard their tale with interest and envy.

"Did ye now? Do they now?" he exclaimed at intervals as they all compared notes about the land, and Mark told Harriet how he had been chariot-racing with Phoebus and Boadicea. "Well, something has cured your cough, lad, whether the sleep or the change of air."

It had. Mark had not coughed once since he had awakened, though Harriet still had a fit of coughing from time to time.

"It is unfair!" she exclaimed, "when I had all the trouble of fetching him back."

They had been arguing about this for some time when they noticed that the doctor and the postman had left the room, and, glancing out of the window, Harriet saw them cross the lawn to the laurel tree. Harriet's clothesline was still dangling from the branches and now, helped by the postman, the doctor hauled himself up by his arms with surprising agility and disappeared into the branches. In a moment the postman followed him. So did the cat, yawning and stretching as it lazily hauled itself up the trunk.

"Hey!" Harriet shouted, leaning from the window, "you mustn't do that! It still isn't safe. . . ."

But they were gone, and when the children ran out and stood under the tree they could hear only contented snores coming from the upper branches.

The Stolen Quince Tree

Harriet was sitting alone upstairs in the dormer window over the porch. There was an old basket chair and a shelf full of entrancing books: *Jackanapes*, *The Silver Skates*, the *Curdie* books, and many others with thick, glossy old bindings and gold lettering. The afternoon sun shone in and made a pinkish patch on the floor. Harriet felt drowsy and comfortable. The remains of whooping cough were still troublesome and kept her awake at nights; Granny had said that she must rest for at least an hour after lunch, from two to three. She was resting now, while Mark practiced archery somewhere in the garden.

Granny had gone off to call on Mrs. Cheevy, and Nursie was at her weekly Women's Institute meeting, so Harriet was in command. It was nice, she thought, to hear the aged house stretching itself and creaking a little around her; the only thing she did wish was that Granny kept a cat, a comfortable tabby or marmalade to stretch beside her in the patch of sunshine and let out a friendly purr from time to time.

Cars passed occasionally in the lane below Granny's ten brick front steps, but they never stopped. All Granny's friends were very, very old and exchanged letters with her in crabbed, trembling handwriting, but they never came calling. Now, however, to Harriet's surprise, a large glossy car did draw up outside the white gate, and a lady jumped out of it and came purposefully up the steps, calling back a remark to someone in the car as she did so.

"Oh, bother," Harriet thought, "now the bell will ring and I shall have to answer it."

She waited. The bell rang.

Uncoiling herself with reluctance from the squeaking chair (which had left basket marks all over her legs), she went downstairs, absentmindedly stepping over the patch of sunshine where the cat should have been lying.

The lady was standing outside the glass-paned front door, looking inquisitively about her. She had on a most interesting hat, Harriet noticed, flowerpot-shaped and made of reddish furry material; out from under its brim curled green-and-white tendrils of Busy Lizzie, which then turned round and climbed up the sides of the hat. The lady's pale, smiling eyes peered from underneath this in rather an odd way.

"Well, little girl," the lady said, and Harriet took an instant dislike to her, "is your mummy in?"

"She doesn't live here," Harriet said politely, "this is my grandmother's house."

"I *see*," the lady said. "Well, may I see *her* then?" She spoke with a hint of impatience.

"I'm afraid everyone is out except me."

"Oh, dear," said the lady, smiling, "then I shall have to explain to you. You see, the fact is I am Miss Eaves, Wildrose Eaves, and I have been looking everywhere, but *every*where for a quince tree. Well! I was driving along this lane and I looked up, and I said to myself, 'There's my quince tree!' So I came straight up here to ask if I could buy it."

"Do you mean," said Harriet doubtfully, "buy Granny's quince tree? Or do you want to buy some quinces? Because I don't think they'll be ripe for a few days, but we could let you know when we pick them."

"No, dear," said Miss Eaves patiently, "I want to buy the *tree*."

"I'm sure Granny would never think of selling the whole tree," said Harriet decidedly. "For one thing, wouldn't it die? And she's very very fond of it, I know—"

"I can see you don't quite understand, dear. I am Wildrose Eaves, *the* Wildrose Eaves, you know."

Harriet plainly didn't know, so the lady explained that she wrote a very famous column, which appeared in a Sunday paper every week, about gardening. "And people all over the world, you see, know every inch and corner of my mossy old garden just from reading about it in the *Sunday Tidings*."

"How nice," Harriet said.

"Well it *would* have been nice, dear, if there *was* such a garden, but the fact is the whole thing was made up. But now I've had this very tempting offer from an American magazine which wants to come and take pictures of it, so you see I'm quickly putting the whole thing together, my charming old cottage, Shadie Thatch, and the yew hedges and pansy beds, but the one thing I couldn't get hold of was a quince tree, and that's very important because I've mentioned it more than once."

"Couldn't you say it had died?"

"Oh, no, dear. Nothing in the garden at Shadie Thatch ever dies."

"Well," said Harriet, "I'm afraid it's not at all likely that Granny will want to sell the tree, but I'll tell her about it. Perhaps you could ring her up about teatime?"

"Tell her I'll pay her five hundred pounds for the tree—with its quinces on naturally. That's most important," said the lady, and she ran down the steps again to her shiny car.

"I never heard such nonsense," said Granny when she came home and Harriet had made her put on her hearing aid and pay attention to the matter. "Sell the quince tree! Whatever next? The woman's a fool, and about as shady as her thatch, from the sound of her."

When the telephone rang, Granny stamped off to give Miss Eaves a piece of her mind. Harriet heard her shouting, "I wouldn't take five hundred pounds nor yet five thousand. And that's my last word; no, certainly not, I shouldn't dream of it." And she rang off vigorously.

"Why," she went on, coming back and picking up her knitting, "your grandpapa planted that tree the year we were married, and I've made quince jam from it for the last fifty years. The impertinence of her! But it's all the same nowadays—people think they can have all the benefits without doing any work for them."

And then it was time for supper and shortly after that time for Harriet and Mark to go to bed.

The children generally woke early in the morning, and if it

was fine, they got up, took biscuits from the pantry, and went out riding. There were two fat, lazy ponies called Dapple and Gray who lived in the paddock at the bottom of the orchard and whose job it was to pull the roller over Granny's wide lawns, wearing felt slippers on their little hoofs. The children were allowed to ride the ponies, and although they could seldom be persuaded out of a jiggling trot, it was a nice thing to do before breakfast. So next morning Harriet and Mark put on their jeans, went down through the orchard, caught the ponies with a bait of sugar, and took them up across the lawn to a side gate leading into the lane.

"We could go to Cloud Bottom," Mark was saying as they came round the corner of the house. "We haven't—good heavens, look!"

They both stared in astonishment and horror. For where, yesterday, the quince tree had grown, beautiful with its rusty leaves and golden fruit, this morning there was nothing but a huge, trampled, earthy hole.

"Tire marks," said Mark, "and big ones. Someone's been here with a truck or a big van."

"The beasts!" exclaimed Harriet. "That beastly woman! I thought she looked sly. Now what are we going to do?"

"I wonder how long they've been gone?"

"Granny'll be most dreadfully upset when she finds out."

"It's still jolly early," said Mark, looking at his watch, "and they can't have dug it up in the dark. I bet they haven't gone far yet. Let's follow the tracks and see if we can find which way they went. Do you remember where the woman said she lived?"

"Didn't give an address," Harriet said gloomily.

They mounted and went out into the lane. It was easy to see from the tire marks and broken bushes where the truck had backed in, and a trail of snapped twigs showed which way it had gone. Luckily the lane was a muddy one, and where it widened, the tread marks showed plainly. The children kicked Dapple and Gray into a sort of amble, their fastest gait, and went on like bloodhounds. They hadn't much idea what they would do if they caught up with the thieves, but they did feel very strongly that the tree must be put back before Granny discovered its loss.

"Remember the time when the black-marketeers stole the holly from the two round bushes?" Mark asked Harriet. "She was quite ill. Goodness knows what this would do to her."

"And the time when the little pippin tree died," Harriet said, nodding. "I say, look over there!"

The lane curved round a couple of meadows, and across the tops of three hedges they could see what looked like a big removal van, stationary at the edge of a little wood.

"I bet it's them," said Mark. "We must make a plan."

They cut across the fields, skirted the wood, and came out into the lane on the far side of the van. Here there were no tire marks. "It's them all right," pronounced Mark. "We'd better send the ponies home—they may have seen them when they were taking the tree."

They dismounted and thumped off Dapple and Gray across the fields in the direction of home.

"Now you must limp," Mark said.

Harriet picked out two or three good sharp flints from the mud in the lane and put them in her shoes. She never did things by halves. Then they went on towards the van, which was still not moving. They saw two men sitting on the road bank, smoking.

The children walked slowly towards them, Harriet hobbling and clutching Mark's elbow.

"Up early, aren't you?" said one of the men. "What's the matter? Little girl hurt her foot?"

"I think I've sprained it," gasped Harriet.

"Could you possibly give us a lift?" said Mark. "I don't think she ought to walk on it."

"Where do you live?" asked one of the men.

"Lower Little Finching," answered Mark, inventing quickly.

"Never heard of it. We're going to Gorsham."

"Oh, that would be fine. You could put us off at Gorsham crossroads."

The men finished their cigarettes and stood up, moving slowly towards the van. It was the usual enormously high furniture removal van, and said simply SMITHS REMOVALS AND STORAGE on its side. Mark noticed with suppressed excitement that a couple of rusty leaves were jammed at the bottom of the roll-down steel back. He wanted to draw Harriet's attention to this but didn't dare.

"Lift the little girl in, Weaver," said the shorter man. "I want to check the fuel."

When he started, he said, "First garage we see I must stop for juice. Only half a gallon left. All that winching used a lot."

The other man scowled at him in a silencing way. So they've got a winch inside there, thought Mark, run by a belt-drive off the engine. He had been wondering how they had gotten the tree out of the ground and into the van.

The driver edged his way cautiously along the narrow track, which was called Back Lane because it swung out in a semi-circle behind the village and then joined the main road again farther along. Just past this road junction was Smalldown Garage, and Ken Clement, who owned it, was a friend; it was Ken who came and mowed Granny's lawn with her crazy, temperamental old motor mower.

"I'll pull in here," said the driver, when he saw Ken's sign.

"How about a bit of breakfast?" suggested Weaver, noticing that the sign also said Snacks.

"Okay. You want any breakfast, kids?"

"No, thank you," said Mark, who was afraid that Ken would ruin things by greeting them. "We've had ours." He wished it were true.

"Well, we shan't be long. You can stay in the cab if you want."

Both men jumped out, and the driver called to Ken, who was hosing down a van, and asked him to fill up the tank. Then they went in at the café door which was round the side of the garage, out of sight.

"Now," said Mark to Harriet, "you must go in and distract their attention. Make a noise, play tunes on the jukebox or something, and don't forget to limp."

Harriet hobbled off. Her foot was really sore by now, she didn't have to pretend. In the café a fat girl was just giving the men plates of bacon and eggs. Luckily Harriet did not know her.

Harriet bought some chocolate and then limped across and put sixpence into the jukebox which jerked and rumbled once or twice and began to play a rather gloomy song:

> "If she bain't a pal to me
> What care I whose pal she be?"

"Oh, blimey!" said Weaver. "I never can hear that song without crying."

"Why?" asked the other man.

"It reminds me so of the missus."

"Well, she's at home waiting for yer, isn't she?"

"Yes, that's just what I mean!" Sure enough, his face was all creased sideways, like a cracker that is just going to be pulled, and as the song went on its gloomy way, he fairly burst out boohooing.

"Here, shall I turn the perishing thing off?"

"Oh, no, Fred, don't do that. It's lovely—makes me feel ever so sad. Put in another sixpence and let's have it again. You don't hear it often nowadays."

"Lumme," said Fred, "there's no accounting for tastes." But he kindly put in another sixpence and started the tune again when it ended, while Weaver sat happily crying into his eggs.

Harriet went quietly out.

"It's all right," she said to Mark, who was waiting round in front. "They're good for another twenty minutes."

"That should do us; come on quick, Ken's waiting. He filled the tank and we had a look inside (lucky thing that twig stuck out, it stopped the lock from engaging properly) and it's our tree all right."

They ran. Ken was in the cab of the van already, and his son Laurie was in the back; Harriet and Mark piled in with Laurie. As Ken pulled out, his other son Tom ran a tractor across the forecourt with a deafening roar that effectively drowned out the noise of their own departure.

It seemed queer to be riding along in a van with a quince tree. A few of the quinces had fallen off, but not so many as might have been expected.

"Must be a very well-sprung van," Mark said.

"Proper shame, though, to take your Granny's quince tree like that," Laurie said. "Why not tell the police?"

"Oh, I expect those men were just hired to do the job.

The main thing is to get it back before Granny notices."

"Ar," Laurie said, "it's going to be a rare old fetch-me-round getting her out and back in the ground. Lucky there's this here crane on board."

They could feel the bumpy, slower progress as Ken edged the van up the lane, and the occasional swish of a branch against the sides. Then he stopped, turned, and backed into Granny's orchard gate.

Laurie stood up and prepared to jump out. "Cor," he said, "a blooming pusscat. Where did she come from?"

They all noticed the cat for the first time. She was sitting in the quince tree looking at them somewhat balefully—a big tortoise-shell with pale green eyes. Harriet was rather upset to notice also that the red flowerpot hat that had so much attracted her attention to Miss Eaves' head was lying at the foot of the tree.

"Do you think it's her?" she asked apprehensively. "Miss Eaves? Now I come to think of it she did look as if she might be a witch."

"If so, why go to the trouble of hiring a van to steal the tree?" Mark answered.

"She couldn't take it across running water."

"That's true," Mark said. "Well, to be on the safe side, we'd better stow her somewhere out of harm's way."

"I'll take her." Harriet clasped the cat firmly around its middle and tucked the red hat under her arm. Then she blushed, thinking how unsuitable this treatment was for the dignified Miss Eaves. If it *was* Miss Eaves.

"Still, it was jolly mean to steal Granny's tree," she said to the cat.

There were lots of unfurnished rooms at the back of Granny's house, apple rooms, onion rooms, tomato rooms, herb rooms and chutney rooms. Harriet shoved the reluctant cat into an apple room with a saucer of water, shut the door and window carefully, and raced back to the others. There was no stirring in the house. It was still very early.

Ken had backed the van right up to the edge of the hole, and they had pulled down a ramp and were now swinging out a movable crane attached to one of the inside walls. The crane's padded clutch was still holding onto the quince tree's trunk, which was all wrapped in felt for protection. Ken got back into the cab and started the engine, and the crane cable tightened and began to throb. The quince tree lurched slightly.

Ken jumped out again. "You kids get in the back there and push," he said, "Laurie, pass this rope round the tree and swing her if she goes askew. I'll work the crane."

Little by little the tree slid forward along the polished steel floor of the van and began to slither down the ramp. The roots, which had been pressed up against the walls, sprang out straight.

"Handy little gadget that crane is, in a furniture van," Laurie said, giving the rope a tug and wiping his face with an earthy hand. "Now we're going to have fun though, getting her back in the hole."

It wasn't so bad as he feared—the hole was far larger than the tree needed and it was just a case of tumping it up and down to make sure the roots were all comfortable. Then, working like beavers, they piled the earth back into the hole and trampled it down.

"It looks terrible," Harriet said. "As if wild bulls had been here."

"Turf, that's what we want," said Laurie. "This here grass'll take a month of Sundays to come back."

"Turf down by the cricket pavilion," said his father. "We was just going to renew the pitch. The club won't begrudge old Mrs. Armitage half a load."

They swung the crane inboard again, hauled down the back (Mark jammed a twig in at the bottom, just as it had been before), and all piled into the cab. Ken hustled the van back down the lane to the garage.

Tom was still exercising his tractor in the forecourt. He gave them a reassuring wave. "Haven't come out yet," he shouted.

Sure enough, when Harriet tiptoed to the café window and peered in, the two van men were still drinking tea, and Weaver was crying while he listened to a tune that went:

> "Oh, breathe not her name
> Or don't breathe it often—"

Later, she often wondered how long it was before they discovered that the tree had gone.

Meanwhile Ken had collected a load of turf from the cricket pitch and took it back in the tractor-trailer. Mark and Harriet rode back with him and helped pack the turfs around the foot of the quince tree, working outwards until they met the unspoiled grass.

"Lucky it was lawn underneath," Ken said, "and not rose garden or summat. That wouldn't have been so easy to fake. Now you fetch the ponies and we'll give the turf a good old flattening."

"We'd better have the quinces picked as quickly as possible," Harriet remarked as they laced on the ponies' felt slippers and harnessed them to the roller, "in case Miss Eaves has another try. Once the quinces are off, the tree isn't any use to her."

"I noticed the telephone linesmen as we were coming through the village from the pavilion," Mark said. "I'll ask them to come and help."

The linesmen always helped Granny pick her fruit, and when they heard Mark's story, they said they would be along with their ladders right away. Ken said he supposed he had better go back and look after the business, and he drove off, waving aside the thanks of Mark and Harriet.

"Never thought she'd look so good," he shouted. The ponies were shuffling round and round with the roller, and the grass beneath the tree had begun to look as if it had been there all its life. A few leaves and one more quince had fallen.

"Well, us'll make a start," said the leader of the telephone men.

"I'll just go and tell Granny you're here," said Harriet. "It's ten minutes to breakfast time."

Granny was delighted to hear that the men had begun on the quinces; she said ever since that woman had called, she had been thinking about quince chutney. As soon as breakfast was over, without even going out to look at the tree, she got out a cook book and a caldron, told Nursie to make some strong tea with molasses in it for the men, and instructed the children to bring in all the quinces that had been picked.

Soon the house was full of the aromatic scent of Granny's quince, tomato, and onion chutney, and Mark and Harriet were kept busy peeling, chopping, and running to and fro with more supplies, while old Nursie doddered around ordering everybody about and taking the men enormous jam tarts.

"Do you think the tree will be all right?" Harriet said to Mark as they stood watching the last of the quinces come down.

"Oh, I should think so," he said. "That's that; now we can let Miss Eaves out. If it *is* Miss Eaves."

Harriet ran indoors with the last basketful.

"Put them in the quince room, child," said Granny, stirring away at her pungent brew. "And then come back and have a good sniff at this steam; it will cure your cough. By the way—"

"Oh!" exclaimed Harriet, stopping on the kitchen hearth. "How did *she* get here?"

"I was going to ask you that," said Granny mildly. "I heard her mewing in the apple room. She's not one of the village cats."

Miss Eaves was sitting comfortably on the hearthstone, washing her tortoise-shell paw with a pink tongue. If it *was* Miss Eaves. How had she mewed loud enough to penetrate Granny's deafness, Harriet wondered.

"I've been wanting a cat," Granny went on. "Ever since old Opussum went to sleep in the laurel tree, the mice have been getting at the codlins. So I buttered her paws and I shall keep her—unless, of course, anyone turns up to claim her."

Harriet was rather taken aback, but Miss Eaves looked uncommonly placid and pleased with herself. An empty sardine saucer stood at one side of the hearth.

After she had had her good sniff at the quince steam (which did indeed cure her cough), Harriet ran off to consult Mark.

"If she's had her paws buttered," he said gloomily, "she'll probably never leave of her own accord. We shall have our work cut out to get rid of her."

And certainly a tactful taking of Miss Eaves to the boundary hedge and dropping her over it did nothing to dislodge her; there were so many windows kept open in Granny's house that Miss Eaves could always get in one or another of them and turn up purring in time for the next meal. Meanwhile, to the children's relief, the quince tree showed no signs of ill effects from its upheaval.

On Nursie's next W.I. afternoon, Granny was making quince honey in the kitchen when Harriet saw the Brushitoff Brush man drive up to the door.

"Do you want any brushes today, Granny?" Harriet shouted through the steam. "The brush man's here."

"No, child. Last week we had an onion brush, the week before a tomato brush, and the week before that a tin of apple polish. Nothing this week, tell him, thank you."

On the way to the front door Harriet found Mark and hissed her plan to him, also borrowing all the money he had, which was sevenpence.

"Granny doesn't want anything, thank you," she said to the man, "but may I look at what you've got. I want to buy a—a present."

The Brushitoff man rapidly undid his suitcase and spread out a most multifarious display of brushes—straight, curved, circular, pliable, stiff, nylon, bristle, sponge, and all colors of the rainbow.

"Oh, how lovely," Harriet said admiringly. "Gracious, isn't it hard to decide. How much is that one?"

"Three and sixpence, miss."

"And this?"

"Five and eleven."

"Oh dear, they do cost a lot, don't they? How much is this little one?"

"Two and six."

Harriet went on hopefully digging in the suitcase. She tried out a muff brush on her cuff and a pot-plant swab on her finger tip. Finally, after much thought, she purchased a tiny button brush that cost only a shilling. The man collected all the other brushes together and drove off in his van.

"Well," said Harriet, meeting Mark breathless on the path outside, "did you do it?"

Mark nodded. "Took Miss Eaves round out the back door and popped her in the van."

"Loose?"

"No, I put her in an empty apple-polish carton. She'll get out in half an hour or so."

"That should be enough," said Harriet, satisfied.

They hoped they had heard the last of Miss Eaves.

Next morning though, at breakfast, Granny sat looking very puzzled over a letter on lavender-colored writing paper on which the printed heading "Wildrose Eaves" nestled among a cluster of forget-me-nots.

"Most extraordinary," said Granny suspiciously, "here's some woman writing to thank me for her delightful visit when to the best of my knowledge she's never been near the place. Says how much she's looking forward to another visit. Must be mad—isn't Eaves the name of the person who wanted my quince tree?"

In fact, it soon appeared that Miss Eaves found catching mice in Granny's apple rooms much more to her taste than writing untruthful gardening articles for the *Sunday Tidings*. After three days she was back again, purring beside the kitchen stove, and the children gave up trying to persuade her to go away, though Harriet never really became accustomed to waking up and finding a lady journalist who was also a witch sleeping on the end of her bed.

"Dear me," Granny said, some weeks after the children had gone back to school, "there must have been a gale one night recently. That quince tree has blown completely around.

The big branch used to be on the south side. And I never heard a thing, not a thing. Just fancy that, puss."

But Miss Eaves, purring round her ankles, said nothing, and Granny strolled on to look at the medlar tree, murmuring, "I'm getting very old; very, very old, puss; very, very old."

A *Batch of Magic Wands*

"What's all this?" said Mr. Armitage, coming down one morning to find the dining room littered with collecting boxes and trays full of blue paper cornflowers.

"Cornflower day," said Mrs. Armitage.

"So I had inferred," replied her husband patiently. "But what's it in aid of?" He peered at some posters lying half unrolled on the floor, which showed a sweet, pathetic old face under a steeple-crowned hat.

"It's to raise money for a bazaar."

"Yes?"

"And the bazaar is to raise money for a progressive whist drive which is to raise money for a garden fête."

"So far, so good," said Mr. Armitage, stepping over his daughter, Harriet, who was counting cornflowers, and helping himself to porridge. "And what's the garden fête in aid of?"

"The S.A.D.O.F.L., of course."

"And that is?"

"The Society for the Aid of Distressed Old Fairy Ladies."

"Do you expect to raise much for them?"

"Oh, yes," said Mrs. Armitage confidently. "Last year we made a terrible lot for the N.S.P.C.M.—enough to provide a warm swimming bath for rheumatic mermaids *and* a beach canteen serving them with hot soup and fish rolls throughout the winter months."

"Most praiseworthy." Mr. Armitage shuddered a little at the thought of the fish rolls and hurriedly took some bacon.

"So we expect to be able to do something of the sort this year. There's a slight difference of opinion on the committee unfortunately; some people want a free dispensary for magical ingredients—eye of newt and toe of frog, you know, and belladonna and so forth; but some committee members think that ought to come under the National Health Service anyway, and that we should write to our Member of Parliament about it."

"So what do they want?"

"A mobile library of magical reference books and free replacements of worn-out wands."

"Well, it all sounds very fine," said Mr. Armitage, gulping down the last of his coffee and preparing to rush off, for this was his office day; "provided you think these people *deserve* to be helped."

"Oh, yes, darling, poor old things! Have you finished counting those out, Harriet? Here come the other helpers, and we must be off."

The flower sellers were beginning to crowd the front hall.

Mrs. Armitage gave each of them a set of one tray, a collection box and a poster. She took the last set herself and, with Harriet, started off along her own beat, between the post office and the green.

At first all went excellently. Heads were shaken and sighs heaved over the plight of the poor, resourceless old fairy ladies in want of comforts. Money flowed in, the tin box became heavier and heavier, until by eleven o'clock it was nearly full.

They were approaching a small cottage, set back from the road among apple trees. It was called The Bat's Nest, and in it lived old Mr. Grogan, with his housekeeper, old Miss Hooting. Mr. Grogan made dolls' furniture. He was stone deaf and hardly talked to anyone except Miss Hooting, who had a very shrill voice which he could just hear. If anyone wanted dolls' furniture, they came and told Miss Hooting their requirements: the size, period, design, and materials wanted. She would pass the information on to Mr. Grogan, and in due course the article would arrive, very beautifully made. Harriet had a Queen Anne walnut chest of drawers with brass handles, of his workmanship, and also a rosewood grand piano, its tiny keys made from spillikins, which really played. Miss Hooting, as well as looking after Mr. Grogan, kept what was thought to be a hen-battery and sold the eggs. She also made hats and did weaving.

"I do admire Miss Hooting," people often said.

When Harriet and her mother came up to the cottage, they saw Miss Hooting walking down the garden path towards the battery-shed, and as they knew it would be useless to apply to Mr. Grogan, they went round to intercept her.

"Good morning," she said in her creaking voice. "Would you like to see me feed my birds?"

"Oh, yes, please," said Harriet.

"What do you give them?" inquired Mrs. Armitage.

"Pellets," replied Miss Hooting, opening a bin which contained tiny whitish balls and shoveling some of them into two buckets. "Now they are tipped into these containers, so, and I pull the rope to raise them to roof level. Now we can go inside."

As she opened the door into the battery, which was dark, pandemonium broke loose.

"Those don't sound like hens," said Mrs. Armitage, puzzled.

"Hens? Who said they were hens?"

There was a squawking and a screeching, a hooting and a snoring.

"I'll have to switch on the light," said Miss Hooting, and did so. The birds immediately became quiet in their little cages and sat watching her with great round eyes.

"Goodness," said Mrs. Armitage in surprise. "They're owls. Do you sell the eggs?"

"Yes, to Sorcerers' Supply Stores. They collect the eggs once every six months or so—owls' eggs don't have to be fresh."

She pulled the two pellet containers through the hatches, and the visitors saw that the containers ran on wheels along two little overhead railways. When they were pushed, they trundled the whole length of the battery, tipping off a portion of food into each owl's cage. The owls bounced up and down with excitement, but kept quiet.

"Now," said Miss Hooting, dusting her hands, "you are collecting, are you not? For some worthy cause, no doubt, but I haven't got my spectacles or my purse, so we must go indoors, and I will also show you the bit of weaving I am engaged on."

They followed her back to the house and into a front room which smelled strongly of raffia, wool, artificial flowers and basket canes, all of which were lying about in large quantities by a large loom.

"Oh," said Harriet in admiration, "what lovely stuff!" The piece of cloth on the loom was not at all the sort of hand-woven stuff she had expected to see. It was a thick, rich-looking red velvet with a black and gold design woven through it.

"It's for a cloak," explained Miss Hooting carelessly, coming back with her bag and glasses. "There's the hat to match." She nodded at a black steeple-crowned one lying beside the bunch of red ribbons which was to trim it. "Now what is it you are collecting in aid of?"

"The S.A.D.O.F.L.," said Mrs. Armitage. "For helping old fairy ladies of various kinds. When they're old, they often get a bit past their work, and we ought to do a bit for them. This is going to a fund for replacing worn-out wands and things of that sort. Gracious, is something the matter?"

Miss Hooting had gone perfectly pale with rage.

"The impertinence!" she exclaimed. "The barefaced, unparalleled effrontery of coming here and saying that to *me!* I suppose you did it as a deliberate insult."

"No, indeed," said Mrs. Armitage, much bewildered. "I certainly had no such intention."

"Fiddlestick! I suppose you'll say next you didn't *know* I was a retired enchantress (fairy lady, indeed). I am not in the least distressed, I'll have you know. I have my pension, my salary from Mr. Grogan, besides what I make from my owls and handicrafts. I am hard-working and self-respecting, and there are plenty more like me who won't say thank you for your charity. The door is behind you. *Good* morning."

Unfortunately, at that moment Mr. Grogan came downstairs, having heard Miss Hooting's voice raised in rage. He rather liked Mrs. Armitage and Harriet, so he said good morning to them and asked Miss Hooting what they had come for.

"Impertinence!" she screeched.

"Yes I dare say, but what sort of furniture?"

"*Not* furniture. They are collecting for a most offensive cause."

"Chest of drawers? Yes, I can do a chest of drawers, but what period?"

"*Not* a chest of drawers, an appeal."

"Made of deal? Never touch the stuff."

Harriet and Mrs. Armitage felt that if they did not leave, Miss Hooting might do something drastic—she was casting meaningful looks at a tall black stick leaning against the mantelpiece. If it was a wand, they thought it would be prudent not to chance the possibility of its not yet being worn out, so, nodding and smiling at Mr. Grogan, they escaped.

When the contents of the various collecting boxes were added together, the total sum was found to be quite a handsome one, though several of the collectors had had unfortunate experiences, like that of the Armitages, with innocent-seeming old ladies.

Mr. Armitage shook his head when he heard about it.

"I should leave the whole affair alone, if I were you," he said. "Buy a grand piano for the Ladies' Social Club, or a machine gun for the Boy Scouts, or something harmless. It's always better to collect for a charity that's a long way off, in

Africa or somewhere like that, if you must. These old fairy ladies are devilish touchy and independent, and there's sure to be trouble."

He was an obliging man, however, and he consented to say a few words to open the bazaar which was due to follow in three weeks, because he said he might not make such a hash of it as the vicar.

Everyone was working early and late making things for the stalls—cakes, embroidered milk-bottle covers, tea-cozy cases, jam-pot containers, bags to put dusters in and bags to put those bags in, dolls with crinolines to put over the coal-scuttle, and crocheted chocolate-bar containers. There was also to be a jumble stall, and all the village flocked to the bazaar in the hope of picking up cheaply the clothes of the children next door which they had been despising and condemning as unsuitable for the past year.

Mr. Armitage stood on the platform to say his opening words, supported by his wife and the members of the committee.

"Good afternoon, ladies and gentlemen," he began, spurred on to rashness by several cups of very strong tea which he had just drunk. "We are all assembled here to enjoy ourselves (I hope) and to raise money for all the poor old distressed fairy ladies living round about. Well now, let's give the poor old things a big hand and buy everything in sight, however nasty or useless it appears to be—"

Here he paused with his mouth open, for several old ladies near the front of the hall were standing up and looking at him in a very unfriendly way. Old Mrs. Lomax was pointing her stick at him.

"Hush, man, hush," she croaked:

"By the magic of this wand,
Be a tadpole in a pond."

Nothing happened.

"*You're* no use," said old Mrs. Lockspith acidly. "You're one of the ones they need to help, evidently." She pointed a long Malacca cane at the speechless Mr. Armitage, and exclaimed:

"Powers of witchcraft in this cane,
Turn him to a drop of rain."

Nothing happened.

"Here, this is ludicrous," said Miss Hooting furiously. "It's my turn. You ladies are a disgrace to the profession." She grabbed her own black staff, leveled it at the platform and recited:

"Enough of useless spells and wasted words,
Turn Armitage and wife to ladybirds."

There was a hush, as the people in the audience craned over one another's shoulders to see if the spell had worked this time, and then a spontaneous burst of applause. Miss Hooting bowed haughtily and left the hall.

On the platform the remaining committee members gazed at one another blankly across a gap. Then the vicar, peering longsightedly at the floor, remarked: "Ah! What a fortunate thing that I have my collecting box with me."

He took it from his pocket, tipped out a hummingbird hawk moth and placed in the box the two ladybirds, who were dazedly crawling about the floor.

"Perhaps I'd better take charge of those," suggested Harriet, coming up. "They'll want to go home, I expect." Secretly, she was a little afraid that the vicar, who was notoriously absent-minded, might forget that there was anything special about the ladybirds and add them to his collection.

She and Mark left the bazaar (which went on swimmingly after such an eventful start and netted two hundred pounds) and took their parents home. They put the ladybirds in a shoe box with some biscuit crumbs and drops of hot sweet tea (for shock) and sat down to discuss the situation.

"Perhaps it's the sort of spell that will wear off in due course," said Harriet.

"Not if I know Miss Hooting, and I somehow feel it wouldn't be much use going to her and begging her to take it off," said her brother.

Harriet grinned. "I've got an idea," she said. "But let's wait till tomorrow. After all, it's rather nice and peaceful like this."

Agnes and Mrs. Epis happened to be on holiday that week, so, with nobody at all to bother them, Mark and Harriet had a beautiful evening: they played mah-jongg till ten and listened to records till midnight.

After next day's breakfast (at which they felt it necessary to eat twice as much as usual and open a pot of strawberry jam to fortify them in their orphaned state), they went and looked into the shoe box.

Much to their surprise they were greeted with a stream of shrill and indignant expostulation. Apparently Mr. and Mrs. Armitage had recovered the use of their voices. The children were scolded for the uncomfortable bedding they had provided and for not bringing breakfast sooner.

"Now, Mark," said Mr. Armitage. "I have a most important conference at my office today—there's a meeting of the World Organization of Agricultural Producers being held there, and I'm the Chairman. So you'll have to take me. Go and put on some presentable clothes, find a nice airy match-box with some cotton wool in it, and you can catch the nine-eighteen. And bring the file of papers on my dressing table."

Mark went off rather gloomily to obey. He had had the best intentions of trying to recover his parents from ladybird-hood, but he had agreed with Harriet that a few days' free-dom from grown-ups would be a pleasant change. Now it seemed that they were going to be more parent-ridden than ever.

"Harriet," Mrs. Armitage was saying. "You'll have to carry me on my National Savings round, and this afternoon I'm going to tea with Mrs. Mildew, so you'll have to take me there. Just give my back a spot of polish will you?"

Harriet complied, thinking regretfully of the day she had planned, riding the unicorn and spring-cleaning her dolls' house.

The nine-eighteen was crowded that morning, but when Mark's fellow passengers observed that a tiny voice was speak-ing to Mark from his breast pocket, they moved well away from him, and at the next stop they all got out.

When Mark and his father reached the office, Miss Choop, the secretary, was sitting on her desk polishing her nails.

"Hello, Sonny," she said condescendingly. "You're in town early. Your Pa's not in yet. Was he at a party last night?"

"Choop!" barked Mr. Armitage, so threateningly that she jumped, and the bottle of nail polish rolled across the floor. "Get off that desk and lay out the agendas for the W.O.A.P. meeting."

"Where is he?" she said fearfully. "I thought I heard his voice, but it was sort of shrill and far away. He's—he's not *haunting* me, is he? I swear I never meant to upset the card index."

"It's all right—he's in here," said Mark comfortingly. "He's been turned into a ladybird. You hurry up and get those things laid out in the Board Room—I can hear people coming."

Members of the World Organization of Agricultural Producers were coming up the stairs, talking in a lot of different languages.

"And where is our esteemed Chairman?" Mr. Svendsen, a tall Swedish farmer, asked Miss Choop.

"He's there," she replied tremulously, indicating the matchbox. Mr. Svendsen raised his eyebrows. They all filed into the Board Room, and Mark took his father's place holding the matchbox. Miss Choop supplied him with an amplifier.

"Order, Gentlemen," said Mr. Armitage shrilly from his perch. "I call upon the Secretary to read the minutes of the last meeting."

Several of the delegates turned pale and asked each other if it was ventriloquism. A Latin-American fainted dead away.

Mr. Armitage was a very efficient Chairman and bustled his meeting through several motions without giving the startled delegates any time for argument.

"Item Six," he said. "Spraying crops of underdeveloped territories from helicopters. Ah, yes, we have received tenders from two different firms manufacturing insecticides, one British, one Russian. Both their prices are about the same, so it remains to be seen which of their products is the more effective."

Heated discussion broke out. It seemed that this was a matter about which the delegates felt very strongly. They shouted in their different languages, gesticulated, and jumped up and down. As far as Mark could make out, the opposing groups were evenly matched.

"There are representatives of the two firms outside with samples of insect powders which they wish to demonstrate," said Miss Choop. "Shall I ask them in?"

"I hope that will not be necessary," said Mr. Armitage hurriedly. "We'll have a vote."

The voting was exactly even.

"As Chairman, I have a casting vote," said Mr. Armitage. "Being British, I naturally give it to the—"

"I demand to have a trial of these powders," cried the Russian delegate. Mr. Armitage was obliged to give in.

Two young men in white coats came in carrying tins of powder, sprays, and little cages of assorted insects.

"This powder produced by my firm," said the first of them, "is guaranteed to destroy any insect life within five hundred cubic meters."

"Six hundred cubic meters," cried the second, putting down his little cage on the table near Mr. Armitage's matchbox. A particularly enormous spider gazed yearningly at Mr. Armitage through the bars. His nerve broke.

"I—I've changed my mind," Mr. Armitage declared. "I think the Osnovskov powder is undoubtedly the better, and it is also a half penny a ton cheaper. I am going to give my casting vote in favor of it."

Both the young men looked greatly disappointed at losing the opportunity to demonstrate their products. The Russian delegate beamed. "Come out to lunch with me," he said. "I shall carry you most carefully, and you shall have a thimbleful of vodka and one grain of caviar."

"Mark, you wait here till I come back," his father instructed him.

Mr. Armitage arrived home in good spirits singing the "Volga Boat Song," but his children were most dispirited.

"I've had an awful day," said Harriet to Mark after supper. "National Savings all morning, and that tea with Mrs. Mildew! Somebody had brought a baby, and it kept grabbing Mother and trying to swallow her."

"We must certainly get them changed back somehow. What was that idea of yours?"

Harriet jumped up. "I thought we'd go and see Mrs. Lomax," she said. "Come on—we'll shut the parents in their shoe box and put them in the meat safe so that they won't come to any harm." This was a most necessary precaution: both Walrus the cat and Alastair the starling had been taking far too much interest in the transformed Armitage parents.

Mark followed her doubtfully. "I don't see that Mrs. Lomax is likely to help," he argued. "She wanted to change Father into a tadpole."

"Yes, but that was before Miss Hooting called her a disgrace to the profession. Think how touchy they are."

Dusk was falling when they reached Cobweb Corner, Mrs. Lomax's bungalow. While they were still at the bottom of the garden, they could hear angry voices, and when they came nearer, they saw Miss Hooting and Mrs. Lomax at opposite sides of the path.

"And if you think I'm going to pay you twenty guineas for that cloak, you're greatly mistaken," Mrs. Lomax was saying furiously. "Who do you think you are, Dior? The hem is five inches off the ground, I shall look a sight. And the hat is too small. I shan't give you a penny more than fifteen. Disgrace to the profession, indeed."

Miss Hooting turned, her face black as thunder, and swept past the children without noticing them.

Mrs. Lomax pointed a walking stick after her and shouted:

"Be a woodlouse," but nothing happened, and she went inside and slammed the door.

Harriet firmly rang the bell, and when the door flew open again, she looked (with some courage) into Mrs. Lomax's furious face.

"Mrs. Lomax," she said. "I know you're not very fond of my family, but I think we might strike a bargain. We want our parents back again, and I expect you'd like a new wand, wouldn't you? That one doesn't seem to be much good. Unfortunately the committee has decided that it's not safe to hand out new wands, so they're all being sent back to the Sorcerers' Supply Stores and there's going to be a free library instead. But I know where they are now, and I expect I could borrow one—just for half an hour or so—if you'd promise to turn our parents back into human beings for us."

Mrs. Lomax looked much more friendly.

"I think that might be arranged," she said. "One can't be too careful over one's associates and I find I have been quite mistaken in my estimate of Miss Hooting's character. If I can repair any harm she has done to your dear parents, I shall be delighted."

"You stay here and talk to her and see she doesn't change her mind," hissed Harriet to Mark. So he chatted politely to Mrs. Lomax and looked at her collection of lizards, while Harriet dashed off to the vicar and begged for the loan of one of the wands which he had stored until they could be despatched back to London.

"Just for half an hour," she pleaded. "While we get Mother and Father changed back. You can't think how we miss them."

"Very well," he agreed. "But please take care. Once in the wrong hands—"

Harriet ran triumphantly back with a heavy ebony stick.
"That should do," said Mrs. Lomax, looking at it professionally, and she recited:

> "O Stick, well-seasoned, elegant and sage,
> Change ladybird and wife to Armitage.

That should do the trick for you." Then she went on, rather hastily:

> "All fairy ladies, from tonight,
> Turn into owls—and serve them right!"

A confused sound of screeching came from the trees. Several owls brushed past them.

"Oh, dear," Harriet said doubtfully, "I don't think the vicar would like—"

A blue flash wriggled up the stick to Mrs. Lomax's hand, she shrank, her eyes became enormous, and all of a sudden she flew off into the trees, crying: "Tu–whit! Tu–whoo!"

"She's turned herself into one, too," said Mark. "She shouldn't have said *all*. Oh, well, let's take the wand back to the vicar."

When they reached home, they found their parents completely restored, but still in the meat safe, very cramped and indignant.

"What were you doing out so late, anyway?" asked Mr. Armitage.

The number of owls about the village was found to have greatly increased, and as a good many old ladies had mysteriously vanished, the proceeds of the progressive whist drive and the garden fête were used to buy a cannon to put in the school playground.

The Apple of Trouble

It was a black day for the Armitage family when Great-uncle Gavin retired. In fact, as Mark pointed out, Uncle Gavin did not exactly retire; he was pushed. He had been High Commissioner of Mbutam-Mbutaland, which had suddenly decided it needed a High Commissioner no longer but would instead become the Republic of Mbutambuta. So Sir Gavin Armitage, K.C.M.G., O.B.E., D.S.O., and so forth, was suddenly turned loose on the world, and because he had expected to continue living at the High Commissioner's Residence for years to come and had no home of his own, he moved in with the parents of Mark and Harriet.

The first disadvantage was that he had to sleep in the ghost's room. Mr. Peake was nice about it; he said he quite understood, and they would probably shake down together very well, he had been used to all sorts of odd company in his three hundred years. But after a few weeks of Great-uncle Gavin's keep-fit exercises, coughing, thumping, har-rumphing, snoring, and blazing open windows, Mr. Peake became quite thin and pale (for a ghost); he migrated through the wall into the room next door, explaining apolo-getically that he wasn't getting a wink of sleep. Unfortunately the room next door was a bathroom, and though Mark didn't mind, Mr. Armitage complained that it gave him the jumps to see a ghostly face suddenly loom up beside his in the

mirror when he was shaving, while Harriet and her mother had to take to the downstairs bathroom, which Mr. Armitage had built onto the house after Mark's outdoor prize bathroom was destroyed by a pair of feuding Druids. Great-uncle Gavin never noticed Mr. Peake at all. He was not sensitive. Besides, he had other things to think about.

One of his main topics of thought was how disgracefully the children had been brought up. He was horrified at the way they were allowed to live all over the house, instead of being pent in some upstairs nursery.

"Little gels should be seen and not heard," he boomed at Harriet, whenever she opened her mouth. To get her out from underfoot during the holidays, he insisted on her enrolling in a domestic science course run by a Professor Grimalkin, who had recently come to live in the village.

As for Mark, he had hardly a minute's peace.

"Bless my soul, boy—" nearly all Great-uncle Gavin's remarks began with this request—"Bless my soul, what are you doing now? *Reading*? Bless my soul, do you want to grow up a muff?"

"A muff, Great-uncle? What is a muff, exactly?" And Mark pulled out the notebook in which he was keeping a glossary of Great-uncle Gavin.

"A muff, why, a muff is a—a funk, sir, a duffer, a frowst, a tug, a swot, a miserable little sneaking *milksop!*"

Mark was so busy writing down all these words that he forgot to be annoyed.

"You ought to be out of doors, sir, ought to be out playin' footer."

"But you need twenty-two people for that," Mark pointed out, "and there's only Harriet and me. Besides it's summer. And Harriet's a bit of a duffer at French cricker."

"Don't be impident, boy! Gad, when I was your age, I'd have been out collectin' birds' eggs."

"Birds' eggs," said Mark, scandalized. "But I'm a subscribing member of the Royal Society for the Protection of Birds."

"Butterflies, then," growled his great-uncle.

"I read a book, Great-uncle, that said all the butterflies were being killed by indiscriminate use of pesticides and what's left ought to be carefully preserved."

Sir Gavin was turning eggplant color and seemed likely to explode.

"Boy's a regular sea-lawyer," he said furiously. "Grow up into one of those confounded trade-union johnnies. Why don't you go out on your velocipede, then, sir? At your age I was as keen as mustard, by gad! Used to ride miles on my penny-farthing, rain or shine."

"No bike," said Mark, "only the unicorn and he's got a swelled fetlock; we're fomenting it."

"Unicorn! Never heard such namby-pamby balderdash in me life! Here," Great-uncle Gavin said, "what's your weekly allowance when your pater's at home?"

With the disturbed family ghost and the prospect of Uncle Gavin's indefinite stay to depress them, Mr. and Mrs. Armitage had rather meanly decided that they were in need of three weeks in Madeira, and had left the day before.

"Half a crown a week," said Mark. "I've had three weeks in advance."

"How much does a bike cost nowadays?"

"Oh, I daresay you could pick one up for thirty-five pounds."

"*What?*" Great-uncle Gavin nearly fell out of his chair, but then, rallying, he pulled seven five-pound notes out of his ample wallet. "Here, then, boy; this is an advance on your allowance for the next two hundred and eighty weeks. I'll collect it from your governor when he comes home. Cut along, now, and buy a bicycle, an' go for a topping spin and *don't let me see your face again till suppertime.*"

"But I don't want a bicycle," Mark said.

"Be off, boy, make yourself scarce, don't argue!—On second thought, 'spose I'd better come with you, to make sure you don't spend the money on some appallin' book about nature."

So Great-uncle Gavin stood over Mark while the latter unwillingly and furiously purchased a super-excellent, low-slung bicycle with independent suspension, disk brakes, three-inch tires, five speeds, and an outboard motor. None of which assets did Mark want in the least, as who would, when they had a perfectly good unicorn to ride?

"Now, be off with you and see how quickly you can get to Brighton and back."

Day after day thereafter, no sooner had he eaten breakfast than Mark was hounded from the house by his relentless great-uncle and urged to try and better his yesterday's time to Brighton.

"Gosh, he must have led those Mbutam-Mbutas a life," Mark muttered darkly in the privacy of Harriet's room.

"I suppose he's old and we ought to be patient with him," Harriet said. She was pounding herbs in a mortar for her domestic science homework.

The trouble was, concluded Mark, gloomily pedaling along one afternoon through a heavy downpour, that during his forty years among the simple savages Great-uncle Gavin had acquired the habit of command; it was almost impossible not to obey his orders.

Almost impossible; but not quite. Presently the rain increased to a cloudburst.

"Drat Great-uncle Gavin! I'm not going all the way to Brighton in this," Mark decided. "Anyway, why *should* I go to Brighton?"

And he climbed a stile and dashed up a short grassy path to a small church nearby which had a convenient, dry-looking porch. He left his bike on the other side of the stile, for that is another disadvantage of bikes: you can never take them all the way to where you want to go.

The church proved to be chilly and not very interesting, so Mark, who always carried a paperback in his pocket, settled on the porch bench to read until the rain abated. After a while, hearing footsteps, he looked up and saw that a small-ish, darkish, foreign-looking man had joined him.

"Nasty afternoon," Mark said civilly.

"Eh? Yes! Yes, indeed." The man seemed nervous; he kept glancing over his shoulder down the path.

"Is your bicycle, boy, by wall yonder?" he asked by and by.

"Yes, it is."

"Is a fine one," the man said. "Very fine one. Would go lickety-spit fast, I daresay?"

"An average of twenty miles per hour," Mark said gloomily.

"Will it? Will it so?"

The little man fell silent, glancing out uneasily once more at the rainy dusk, while Mark strained his eyes to see the print of his book. He noticed that his companion seemed to be shuffling about, taking a pack off his back and rummaging among the contents; presently Mark realized that something was being held out to him. He looked up from the page and saw a golden apple—quite a large one, about the size of a Bramley. On one side the gold had a reddish bloom, as if the sun had ripened it. The other side was paler. Somebody had taken two bites out of the red side; Mark wondered what it had done to their teeth. Near the stalk was a dark-brown stain, like a patch of rust.

"Nice, eh?" the little man said, giving the apple to Mark, who nearly dropped it on the floor. It must have weighed at least four pounds.

"Is it real gold all through?" he asked. "Must be quite valuable?"

"Valuable?" the man said impressively. "Such apple is beyond price. You, of course, well-educated, familiar with Old Testament tale of Adam and Eve?"

"W–why yes," Mark said, stammering a little. "But you— you don't mean to say *that* apple—?"

"Self same one," the little man said, nodding his head. "Original bite marks of Adam and Eve before apple carried out of Eden. Then—see stain? Blood of Abel. Cain killed him for apple. Stain will never wash off."

"Goodness," Mark said.

"Not all, however—not all at all! Apple of Discord—golden apple same which began Trojan War—have heard of such?"

"Why yes. But—but you're not telling me—"

"Identical apple," the little man said proudly. "Apples of Asgard, too? Heard of? Scandinavian golden apples of perpetual youth, guarded by the goddess Idunn?"

"Yes, but you don't—"

"Such was one of those. Not to mention Apples of Hesperides, stolen by Hercules."

"Hold on—surely it couldn't have been both?"

"Could," the little man said. "Was. William Tell's apple— familiar story?—same apple. Newton—apple fell on head letting in dangerous principle of gravity. This. Atalanta—apple thrown by Venus to stop her winning race. Also, Prince Ahmed's apple—"

"Stop, stop!" said Mark. "I don't understand how it could possibly be *all* those." But somehow, as he held the heavy, shining thing in his hand, he did believe the little man's story. There was a peculiar, rather nasty fascination about the apple. It scared him, and yet he wanted it.

"So, see," the little man said, nodding more than ever, "worth millions pounds. No lie—millions. And yet I give to you—"

"Now wait a minute—"

"Give in exchange for bicycle, yes? Okay?"

"Well, but—but *why*? Why don't you want the apple?"

"Want bicycle more." He glanced down the road again, and now Mark guessed.

"Someone's after you—the police? You stole the apple?"

"Not stole, no, no, no! Did swap, like with bicycle, you agree, yes?"

He was already halfway down the path. Hypnotized, Mark watched him climb the stile and mount the bike, wobbling. Suddenly, Mark found his voice and called,

"What did you swap for it?"

"Drink of water—in desert, see?"

"Who's chasing you, then?"

By now the little man was chugging down the road and his last word, indistinct, floated back through the rain, something ending in "—ese"; it might have been Greek for all Mark could make of it.

He put the apple in his pocket, which sagged under the weight, and, since the shower was slackening, walked to the road to flag a lift home in the next truck.

Great-uncle Gavin nearly burst a blood vessel when he learned that Mark had exchanged his new bicycle for an apple, albeit a gold one.

"Did what—merciful providence—an *apple?*—Hesperides? Eden? Asgard? Never heard such a pack of moonshine in all me born—let's see it, then. Where is it?"

Mark produced the apple and a curious gleam lit up Uncle Gavin's eye.

"Mind," he said, "don't believe a word of the feller's tale, but plain that's val'ble; far too val'ble an article to be in *your* hands, boy. Better give it here at once. I'll get Christie's to value it. And of course we must advertise in *The Times* for the wallah who palmed it off on you—highly illegal transaction, I daresay."

Mark felt curiously relieved to be rid of the apple, as if a load had been lifted from his mind as well as his pocket.

He ran upstairs, whistling. Harriet, as usual, was in her room mixing things in retorts and crucibles. When Uncle Gavin, as in duty bound, asked each evening what she had been learning that day in her domestic science course, she always replied briefly, "Spelling." "Spellin', gel? Rum notion of housekeepin' the johnny seems to have. Still, daresay it keeps you out of mischief." In fact, as Harriet had confided to Mark, Professor Grimalkin was a retired alchemist who, having failed to find the Philosopher's Stone, was obliged to take in pupils to make ends meet. He was not a very good teacher; his heart wasn't in it. Mark watched Harriet toss a pinch of green powder into a boiling beaker. Half a peach tree shot up, wavered, sagged, and then collapsed. Impatiently Harriet tipped the frothing liquid out of the window and put some more water on to boil.

Then she returned to the window and peered out into the dark.

"Funny," she said, "there seem to be some people waiting outside the front door. Can't think why they didn't ring the bell. Could you let them in, Mark? My hands are all covered with prussic acid. I expect they're friends of Uncle Gavin's."

Mark went down and opened the door. Outside, dimly illuminated by the light from the porch, he saw three ladies. They seemed to be dressed in old-fashioned clothes, drainpipe skirts down to their ankles, and cloaks and bonnets rather like those of Salvation Army lasses; the bonnets were perched on thick, lank masses of hair. Mark didn't somehow care for their faces, which resembled those of dogs—but not tame domestic dogs so much as starved, wild, slightly mad dogs; they stared at Mark hungrily.

"Er—I'm so sorry? Did you ring? Have you been waiting long?" he said.

"A long, long time. Since the world-tree was but a seed in darkness. We are the Daughters of Night," one of them hollowly replied. She moved forward with a leathery rustle.

"Oh." Mark noticed that she had bats' wings. He stepped back a little. "Do you want to see Great-uncle—Sir Gavin Armitage? Won't you come in?"

"Nay. We are the watchers by the threshold. Our place is here."

"Oh, all right. What name shall I say?"

To this question they replied in a sort of gloomy chant, taking turns to speak.

"We are the avengers of blood."

"Sisters of the nymph with the apple-bough, Nemesis."

"We punish the sin of child against parent—"

"Youth against age—"

"Brother against brother—"

"We are the Erinyes, the Kindly Ones—" (But their expressions were far from kindly, Mark thought.)

"Tisiphone—"

"Alecto—"

"And Megaera."

"And what did you wish to see Sir Gavin about?" Mark knew his great-uncle hated to be disturbed once he was settled in the evening with a glass of port and *The Times*.

"We attend him who holds the apple."

"There is blood on it—a brother's blood, shed by a brother."

"It cries for vengeance."

"Oh, I *see!*" said Mark, beginning to take in the situation. Now he understood why the little man had been so anxious for a bicycle. "But, look here, dash it all, Uncle Gavin hasn't shed any blood! That was Cain, and it was a long time ago. I don't see why Uncle should be responsible."

"He holds the apple."

"He must bear the guilt."

"The sins of the fathers are visited on the children."

"Blood calls for blood."

Then the three wolfish ladies disconcertingly burst into a sort of hymn, shaking tambourines and beating on them with brass-studded rods which they pulled out from among their draperies:

> "We are the daughters
> Of darkness and time
> We follow the guilty
> We punish the crime
> Nothing but bloodshed
> Will settle old scores
> So blood has to flow and
> That blood must be yours!"

When they had finished, they fixed their ravenous eyes on Mark again and the one called Alecto said,

"Where is he?"

Mark felt greatly relieved that Uncle Gavin had taken the apple away from him and was, therefore, apparently responsible for its load of guilt, but as this was a mean thought he tried to stifle it. Turning (not that he liked having the ladies behind his back), he went into the sitting room, where Uncle Gavin was snug by the fire, and said,

"There are some callers asking for you, Great-uncle."

"God bless my soul, at this time of the evenin'? Who the deuce—"

Great-uncle Gavin crossly stumped out to the porch, saying over his shoulder, "Why didn't you ask 'em in, boy? Not very polite to leave 'em standing—"

Then he saw the ladies and his attitude changed. He said sharply,

"Didn't you see the notice on the gate, my good women? It says 'No Hawkers or Circulars.' I give handsome checks to charity each year at Christmas and make it a rule never to contribute to door-to-door collections. So be off, if you please!"

"We do not seek money," Tisiphone hungrily replied.

"Milk-bottle tops, jumble, old gold, it's all the same. Pack of meddlesome old maids—I've no time for you!" snapped Sir Gavin. "Good night!" And he shut the door smartly in their faces.

"Have to be firm with that sort of customer," he told Mark. "Become a thorough nuisance otherwise—tiresome old harpies. Got wind of that golden apple, I daresay—shows what happens when you mix with such people. Shockin' mistake. Take the apple to Christie's tomorrow. Now, please see I'm not disturbed again." And he returned to the sitting room.

Mark looked uneasily at the front door but it remained shut; evidently the three Kindly Ones were content to wait outside. But there they stayed; when Mark returned to Harriet's room he looked out of the window and saw them, sombre and immovable, in the shadows outside the porch, evidently prepared to sit out the night.

"Not very nice if they're going to picket our front door from now on," he remarked gloomily to Harriet. "Goodness knows what the postman will think. And *I* don't fancy 'em above half. Wonder how we can get rid of them."

"I've an idea," Harriet said. "Professor Grimalkin was talking about them the other day. They are the Furies. But it's awfully hard to shake them off once they're after you. Maybe the postman won't see them. They aren't after *him*."

"There must be *some* way of getting rid of them," Mark said glumly.

"There are various things you can do, biting off your finger—"

"Some hope of Uncle Gavin doing that!"

"Or shaving your head."

"Wouldn't be much use since he's bald as a bean already."

"You can bathe seven times in running water or take the blood of pigs—"

"He always *does* take a lot of cold baths and we had pork for supper, so plainly that's no go."

"Well, you can go into exile for a year," Harriet said.

"I only wish he would."

"Or build them a grotto, nice and dark, preferably under an ilex tree, and make suitable offerings."

"Such as what?"

"Anything black, or they rather go for iris flowers. Milk and honey too. And they can be shot with a bow of horn, but that doesn't seem to be very successful as a rule."

"Oh, well, let's try the milk-and-honey and something black for now," Mark said. "And I'll make a bow of horn to-morrow—I've got Candleberry's last year's horn in my room somewhere." Candleberry was the unicorn.

Harriet, therefore, collected a black velvet pincushion and a bowl of milk and honey. These she put out on the front step, politely wishing the Daughters of Night good evening, to which their only response was a baleful silence.

Next morning the milk and honey were still there. So were the Furies. Evidently they did not intend to be placated so easily. By daylight they were even less attractive, having black claws, bloodshot eyes, and snakes for hair. However, slipping down early to remove the saucer in case the postman tripped over it, Harriet did notice that all the pins had been removed from the pincushion. And eaten? This was encouraging. So was the fact that when the postman arrived with a card from their parents in Madeira—*Having wonderful time, hope you are behaving yourselves*—he walked clean through the Furies without noticing them at all.

"Perhaps they're only visible to relatives of their victims," Harriet suggested to Mark, who was working on the unicorn horn with emery paper.

"I hope they've taken the pins to stick in Uncle Gavin," he growled. In default of bicycle exercise Great-uncle Gavin had made Mark do five hundred push-ups before breakfast and had personally supervised the operation. Mark felt it would be far, far better to shoot Uncle Gavin than the Furies, who, after all, were only doing their duty.

The most annoying thing of all was that, after his initial interview with them, Uncle Gavin seemed not to notice the avenging spirits at all ("He only sees what he chooses to," Harriet guessed) and walked past them quite as unconcernedly as the postman had. He packed up the golden apple in a cigar box, rang for a taxi, and departed for London. The Furies followed him in a black, muttering group, and were seen no more for several hours; Mark and Harriet heaved sighs of relief. Prematurely, though; at teatime the Furies reappeared, even blacker, muttering still more, and took up their post once more by the front door.

"Lost the old boy somewhere in London," Mark diagnosed. "Or perhaps they were chucked out of Christie's."

The unwanted guests were certainly in a bad mood. This time they were accompanied by a smallish thickset winged serpent or dragon who seemed to be called Ladon. Harriet heard them saying, "Down, Ladon! Behave yourself, and soon you shall sup on blood." Ladon, too, seemed to have a snappish disposition, and nearly took off Harriet's hand when she stooped to pat him on returning home from her Domestic Science lesson.

"What a beautiful green his wings are. Is he yours?" she said to the Furies politely.

"He is the guardian of the apple; he but waits for his own," Tisiphone replied dourly.

Ladon did not share the Furies' scruples about coming indoors; evidently he was used to a warmer climate and found the doorstep too draughty. He followed Harriet into the kitchen and flopped his bulky length in front of the stove, hissing cantankerously at anyone who came near, and greatly discomposing Walrus the cat.

Walrus was not the only one.

"Miss Harriet! Get that nasty beast out of here at once!" exclaimed Mrs. Epis, the cook, when she came back from shopping. "And what those black ladies are doing out on the front doorstep I'm sure I don't know; I've two or three times give 'em a hint to be off but they won't take it."

Evidently Mrs. Epis counted as one of the family or else she had a guilty conscience. Mark and Harriet soon found that visitors to the house who had episodes in their past of which they had cause to be ashamed were apt to notice the

Erinyes in a patchy, nervous way and hurry away with uneasy glances behind them, or else break into sudden and embarrassing confessions.

And Ladon was a thorough nuisance. As long as Harriet kept on the fan heater in her room, he would lie in front of it rolling luxuriously on his back and only snapping at anyone who approached him. But at bedtime when she turned the fan off—for she hated a warm room at night—he became fretful and roamed snarling and clanking about the house. Even Uncle Gavin tripped over him then and blamed the children furiously for leaving what he thought was a rolled-up tent lying in the passage.

"Things can't go on like this," Mark said despondently.

"We've certainly got to get rid of them all somehow before Mother and Father come home next week," Harriet agreed. "And Uncle Gavin's plainly going to be no help at all."

Uncle Gavin was even more tetchy than usual. Christie's had sent him a letter saying that, in view of the apple's unique historical interest, it was virtually impossible to put a price on it, but in their opinion it was certainly worth well over a million pounds. They would return the apple by the next registered post pending further instructions. And the advertisement which appeared in *The Times* every day, "Will person who persuaded young boy to exchange valuable new bicycle for metal apple on August 20 please contact Box XXX," was producing no replies.

"Nor likely to," said Mark. "That chap knows when he's well out of trouble."

When Mark had finished his horn bow, he tried shooting at the Furies with it. The operation was a total failure. The arrows, which he had decided to make out of slivers from a fallow-deer's antler were curved and flew on a bias, missing the visitors nine times out of ten. If they did hit, they merely passed clean through, and, as Mark told Harriet later, he felt a fool having to pick them up under the malign, snakey-and-bonneted gaze of Alecto, Megaera, and Tisiphone.

Harriet, however, came home in good spirits. She pulled out and showed Mark a paper covered with Professor Grimalkin's atrocious handwriting.

"What is it?" he asked.

"Recipe for a friendship philter. You've heard of a love philter? This is like that, only milder. I'm going to try it in their milk. Now don't interrupt, while I make it up."

She put her crucible on to bubble. Mark curled up at the end of her bed and read his bird book, coming out only when Harriet tripped over Ladon and dratted him, or asked Mark's opinon about the professor's handwriting.

"Is this 'verdigris' or 'verjuice,' do you think? And is that 'Add sugar' or 'Allow to simmer?'"

"It'll be a miracle if the stuff turns out all right," Mark said pessimistically. "Anyway, do we *want* the Furies friendly?"

"Of course we do, it'll be a tremendous help. Where was I now? Add bad egg, and brown under grill."

Finally the potion was finished and put in a cough-mixture bottle. ("It smells awful," Mark said, sniffing. "Never mind," Harriet said, "how do we know what they like?") A spoonful of the noxious stuff was divided between three bowls of milk, which were placed on the front step, at the feet of the unresponsive Erinyes.

However, after a moment or two they began to snuff the air like bloodhounds on the track of a malefactor, and as Harriet tactfully retired, she had the pleasure of seeing all three of them lapping hungrily at the mixture. So far, at least, the spell had worked. Harriet went hopefully to bed.

Next morning she was awakened by a handful of earth flung at her window.

"Miss Harriet!" It was Agnes on the lawn. "Miss Harriet, you'll have to make the breakfast yourself. I'm taking a week's holiday and so's Mrs. Epis. And things had better be different when we come back or we'll give in our notice; and you can tell your Ma it was me broke the Crown Derby teapot and I'm sorry about it, but there's some things that a body can't bear. Now I'm off home."

Sleepy and mystified, Harriet went to the kitchen to put on the kettle for Great-uncle Gavin's tea. There, to her dismay, she found the Furies, who greeted her with toothy smiles. They were at ease in basket chairs round the stove, with their long skirts turned back so as to toast their skinny legs and feet, which rested on Ladon. Roused by the indoor warmth, the snakes on their heads were in a state of disagreeable squirm and writhe, which Harriet, too, found hard to bear, particularly before breakfast; she quite sympathized with the cook's departure.

"Oh, good morning," she said, however, stoutly controlling her qualms. "Would you like some more milk?" She mixed another brew with potion (which was graciously accepted) and took up a tray of breakfast to Great-uncle Gavin, explaining that Mrs. Epis had been called away. By the time she returned, Mark was in the kitchen, glumly taking stock of the situation.

"Feel like a boiled egg?" Harriet said.

"I'll do it, thanks. I've had enough of your domestic science."

They ate their boiled eggs in the garden. But they had taken only a bite or two when they were startled by hysterical screams from the window cleaner who, having arrived early

and started to work on the kitchen window, had looked through the glass and was now on his knees in the flowerbed, confessing to anyone who would listen that he had pinched a diamond brooch from an upstairs bedroom in West Croydon. Before he was pacified, they had also to deal with the electrician who came to mend the fridge and seemed frightfully upset about something he had done to a person called Elsie, as well as a French onion seller, who dropped eight strings of onions in the back doorway and fled crying, "*Mon Dieu, mon Dieu, mon crime est découvert! Je suis perdu!*"

"This won't do," said Mark, as he returned from escorting the sobbing electrician to the gate. Exhaustedly mopping his brow, he didn't look where he was going, barked his shins painfully on Ladon, who was stalking the cat, and let out an oath. It went unheard; the Furies, much cheered by their breakfast and a night spent in the snug kitchen, were singing their bloodthirsty hymn *fortissimo*, with much clashing of tambourines. Ladon and the cat seemed all set for a duel to the death; and Great-uncle Gavin was bawling down the stairs for "less row while a man was breakfastin', dammit!"

"It's all right," Harriet soothed Mark. "I knew the potion would work wonders. Now, Your Kindlinesses," she said to the Erinyes, "we've got a beautiful grotto ready for you, just the sort of place you like, except I'm sorry there isn't an ilex tree, if you wouldn't mind stepping this way," and she led them to the coal cellar, which, being peaceful and dark, met with their entire approval.

"I daresay they'll be glad of a nap," she remarked, shutting the door thankfully on them. "After all, they've been unusually busy lately."

"That's all very well," said Mark. "They'd better not stay

there long. *I'm* the one that fetches the coal. And there's still beastly Ladon to dispose of."

Ladon, unlike his mistresses, was not tempted by milk containing a friendship potion. His nature remained as intractable as ever. He now had Walrus the cat treed on the banister post at the top of the stairs, and was coiled in a baleful bronze-and-green heap just below, hissing like a pressure cooker.

"Perhaps bone arrows will work on *him*," said Mark, and dashed to his bedroom.

As he reappeared, a lot of things happened at once.

The postman rang the front doorbell and handed Harriet a letter for Uncle Gavin and a registered parcel labeled GOLD WITH CARE. Ladon made a dart at the cat, who countered with a faster-than-light left hook, all claws extended. It caught the dragon in his gills, and he let out a screech like the whistle of a steam locomotive, which fetched the Furies from their grotto on the double, brass-studded batons out and snakes ready to strike.

At the same moment Mark let fly with his bow and arrow, and Uncle Gavin burst from his bedroom exclaiming, "I *will* not have this bedlam while I'm digestin' my breakfast!" He received the arrow intended for Ladon full in his slippered heel and gave a yell which quite drowned the noise made by the cat and the dragon.

"Who did that? Who fired that damned thing?" Enraged, hopping, Uncle Gavin pulled out the bone dart. "What's that cat doin' up there? Why's this confounded reptile in the house? Who are those people down there? *What the devil's going on around here?*"

Harriet gave a shout of joy. "Look, quick!" she called to the Furies. "Look at his heel! It's bleeding!" (It was indeed.)

"You said blood had to flow and now it has, so you've done your job and can leave with clear consciences! Quick, Mark, open the parcel and give that wretched dragon his apple and they can *all* leave. Poor Uncle Gavin, is your foot very painful? Mark didn't mean to hit you. I'll bandage it up."

Mark tore the parcel open and tossed the golden apple to Ladon, who caught it with a snap of his jaws and was gone in a flash through the landing window. (It was shut, but no matter.) At the same moment the Furies, their lust for vengeance appeased by the sight of Uncle Gavin's gore, departed with more dignity by the front door.

Alecto even turned and gave Harriet a ghastly smile.

"Thank you for having us, child," she said. "We enjoyed our visit."

"Don't mention it," Harriet mechanically replied, and only just stopped herself from adding, "Come again."

Then she sat her great-uncle in the kitchen armchair and bathed his heel. The wound, luckily, proved to be no more than a scratch. While she bandaged it, he read his letter and suddenly gave a curious grunt, of pleasure and astonishment.

"God bless my soul! They want me back! Would you believe it!"

"Who want you back, Great-uncle?" Harriet asked, tying the ends of the bandage in a knot.

"The Mbutam-Mbutas, bless 'em! They want me to go and help 'em as Military and Economic Adviser. Well, well, well! Don't know when I've been so pleased." He gave his nose a tremendous blow and wiped his eyes.

"Oh, Uncle Gavin, how perfectly splendid!" Harriet hugged him. "When do they want you to go?"

"Three weeks' time. Bless my soul, I'll have a bustle getting me kit ready."

"Oh, we'll all help like mad. I'll run down the road now and fetch Mrs. Epis; I'm sure she'll be glad to come back for such an emergency."

Mrs. Epis had no objection at all, once she was assured the intruders were gone.

Harriet had one startled moment when they got back to the house.

"Uncle Gavin!" she called and ran upstairs. The old gentleman had out his tin tropical trunk and was inspecting a pith helmet. "Yes, m'dear, what is it?" he said absently.

"The little brown bottle on the kitchen table. Was it—did you—?"

"Oh, that? My cough mixture? Yes, I finished it and threw the bottle away. Why, though, bless my soul—there's my cough mixture! What the deuce have I been an' taken, then, gel? Anything harmful?"

"Oh no, perfectly harmless," Harriet hastily reassured him. "Now, you give me anything you want mended and I'll be getting on with it."

" 'Pon me soul," Uncle Gavin said, pulling out a bundle of spotless white ducks and a dress jacket with tremendous epaulets and fringes, " 'pon me soul, I believe I'll miss you young ones when I'm back in the tropics. Come and visit me sometimes, m'dear? Young Mark too. Where is the young rogue? Ho, ho, can't help laughing when I think how he hit me in the heel. Who'd have thought he had it in him?"

"He's gone apple picking at the farm down the road," Harriet explained. "He wants to earn enough to pay back that thirty-five pounds."

"Good lad, good lad!" Uncle Gavin exclaimed approvingly. "Not that he need have bothered, mark you."

And in fact when Mark tried to press the money on Uncle Gavin, he would have none of it.

"No, no, bless your little hearts, split it between you." He chucked Harriet under the chin and earnestly shook Mark's hand. "I'd never have thought I'd cotton to young 'uns as I have to you two—'mazing thing. So you keep the money and buy something pretty to remind you of my visit."

But Mark and Harriet thought they would remember his visit quite easily without that—especially as the Furies had taken quite a fancy to the coal cellar and frequently came back to occupy it on chilly winter nights.

The Serial Garden

"Cold rice pudding for breakfast?" said Mark, looking at it with disfavor.

"Don't be fussy," said his mother. "You're the only one who's complaining." This was unfair, for she and Mark were the only members of the family at table, Harriet having developed measles while staying with a school friend, while Mr. Armitage had somehow managed to lock himself in the larder. Mrs. Armitage never had anything but toast and marmalade for breakfast anyway.

Mark went on scowling at the chilly-looking pudding. It had come straight out of the fridge, which was not in the larder.

"If you don't like it," said Mrs. Armitage, "unless you want Daddy to pass you cornflakes through the larder ventilator, flake by flake, you'd better run down to Miss Pride and get a small packet of cereal. She opens at eight; Hickmans doesn't open till nine. It's no use waiting till the blacksmith comes to let your father out; I'm sure he won't be here for hours yet."

There came a gloomy banging from the direction of the larder, just to remind them that Mr. Armitage was alive and suffering in there.

"*You're* all right," shouted Mark heartlessly as he passed the larder door. "There's nothing to stop *you* having corn-flakes. Oh, I forgot, the milk's in the fridge. Well, have cheese and pickles then. Or treacle tart."

Even through the zinc grating on the door he could hear his father shudder at the thought of treacle tart and pickles for breakfast. Mr. Armitage's imprisonment was his own fault, though; he had sworn that he was going to find out where the mouse got into the larder if it took him all night, watching and waiting. He had shut himself in, so that no member of the family should come bursting in and disturb his vigil. The larder door had a spring catch which sometimes jammed; it was bad luck that this turned out to be one of the times.

Mark ran across the fields to Miss Pride's shop at Sticks Corner and asked if she had any cornflakes.

"Oh, I don't think I have any left, dear," Miss Pride said woefully. "I'll have a look. . . . I think I sold the last packet a week ago Tuesday."

"What about the one in the window?"

"That's a dummy, dear."

Miss Pride's shop window was full of nasty, dingy old card-board cartons with nothing inside them, and several empty display stands which had fallen down and never been propped up again. Inside the shop were a few small, tired-looking tins and jars, which had a worn and scratched appearance as if mice had tried them and given up. Miss Pride herself was small and wan, with yellowish gray hair; she rooted rather hopelessly in a pile of empty boxes. Mark's mother never bought any groceries from Miss Pride's if she could help it, since the day when she had found a label inside the foil wrapping of a cream cheese saying, "This cheese should be eaten before May 11, 1899."

"No cornflakes I'm afraid, dear."

"Any wheat crispies? Puffed corn? Rice nuts?"

"No, dear. Nothing left, only Brekkfast Brikks."

"Never heard of *them*," said Mark doubtfully.

"Or I've a jar of Ovo here. You spread it on bread. That's nice for breakfast," said Miss Pride, with a sudden burst of salesmanship. Mark thought the Ovo looked beastly, like yellow paint, so he took the packet of Brekkfast Brikks. At least it wasn't very big. . . . On the front of the box was a picture of a fat, repulsive, fair-haired boy, rather like the chubby Augustus, banging on his plate with his spoon.

"They look like tiny doormats," said Mrs. Armitage, as Mark shoveled some Brikks into the bowl.

"They taste like them too. Gosh," said Mark, "I must hurry or I'll be late for school. There's rather a nice cut-out garden on the back of the packet though; don't throw it away when it's empty, Mother. Good-by, Daddy," he shouted through the larder door, "hope Mr. Ellis comes soon to let you out." And he dashed off to catch the school bus.

At breakfast next morning Mark had a huge helping of Brekkfast Brikks and persuaded his father to try them.

"They taste just like esparto grass," said Mr. Armitage fretfully.

"Yes I know, but do take some more, Daddy. I want to cut out the model garden, it's so lovely."

"Rather pleasant, I must say. It looks like an eighteenth-century German engraving," his father agreed. "It certainly was a stroke of genius putting it on the packet. No one would ever buy these things to eat for pleasure. Pass me the sugar, please. And the cream. And the strawberries."

It was the half-term holiday, so after breakfast Mark was able to take the empty packet away to the playroom and get on with the job of cutting out the stone walls, the row of little trees, the fountain, the yew arch, the two green lawns, and the tiny clumps of brilliant flowers. He knew better than to "stick tabs in slots and secure with paste," as the directions suggested; he had made models from packets before and knew they always fell to pieces unless they were firmly bound together with transparent sticky tape.

It was a long, fiddling, pleasurable job.

Nobody interrupted him. Mrs. Armitage only cleaned the playroom once every six months or so, when she made a ferocious descent on it and tidied up the tape recorders, roller skates, meteorological sets, and dismantled railway engines, and threw away countless old magazines, stringless tennis rackets, abandoned paintings, and unsuccessful models. There were always bitter complaints from Mark and Harriet; then they forgot and things piled up again till next time.

As Mark worked, his eye was caught by a verse on the outside of the packet:

> "Brekkfast Brikks to start the day
> Make you fit in every way.
> Children bang their plates with glee
> At Brekkfast Brikks for lunch and tea!

Brekkfast Brikks for supper too
Give peaceful sleep the whole night through."

"Blimey," thought Mark, sticking a cedar tree into the middle of the lawn and then bending a stone wall round at dotted lines A, B, C, and D. "I wouldn't want anything for breakfast, lunch, tea, and supper, not even Christmas pudding. Certainly not Brekkfast Brikks."

He propped a clump of gaudy scarlet flowers against the wall and stuck them in place.

The words of the rhyme kept coming into his head as he worked, and presently he found that they went rather well to a tune that was running through his mind, and he began to hum, and then to sing; Mark often did this when he was alone and busy.

"Brekkfast Brikks to sta–art the day,
Ma–ake you fi–it in every way—

"Blow, where did I put that little bit of sticky tape? Oh, there it is.

"Children bang their pla–ates with glee
At Brekkfast Brikks for lunch and tea

"Slit gate with razor blade, it says, but it'll have to be a penknife.

"Brekkfast Brikks for supper toohoo
Give peaceful sleep the whole night throughoo. . . .

"Hullo. That's funny," said Mark.

It was funny. The openwork iron gate he had just stuck in position now suddenly towered above him. On either side, to right and left, ran the high stone wall, stretching away into foggy distance. Over the top of the wall he could see tall trees, yews and cypresses and others he didn't know.

"Well, that's the neatest trick I ever saw," said Mark. "I wonder if the gate will open?"

He chuckled as he tried it, thinking of the larder door. The gate did open, and he went through into the garden.

One of the things that had already struck him as he cut them out was that the flowers were not at all in the right proportions. But they were all the nicer for that. There were huge velvety violets and pansies the size of saucers; the hollyhocks were as big as dinner plates and the turf was sprinkled with enormous daisies. The roses, on the other hand, were miniature, no bigger than cuff buttons. There were real fish in the fountain, bright pink.

"I made all this," thought Mark, strolling along the mossy path to the yew arch. "Won't Harriet be surprised when she sees it. I wish she could see it now. I wonder what made it come alive like that?"

He passed through the yew arch as he said this and discovered that on the other side there was nothing but gray, foggy blankness. This, of course, was where his cardboard garden had ended. He turned back through the archway and gazed with pride at a border of huge scarlet tropical flowers which were perhaps supposed to be geraniums but certainly hadn't turned out that way. "I know! Of course, it was the rhyme, the rhyme on the packet."

He recited it. Nothing happened. "Perhaps you have to sing it," he thought and (feeling a little foolish) he sang it through to the tune that fitted so well. At once, faster than blowing out a match, the garden drew itself together and shrank into its cardboard again, leaving Mark outside.

"What a marvelous hiding place it'll make when I don't

want people to come bothering," he thought. He sang the spell once more, just to make sure that it worked, and there was the high mossy wall, the stately iron gate, and the tree-tops. He stepped in and looked back. No playroom to be seen, only gray blankness.

At that moment he was startled by a tremendous clanging, the sort of sound the Trump of Doom would make if it was a dinner bell. "Blow," he thought, "I suppose that's lunch." He sang the spell for the fourth time; immediately he was in the playroom, and the garden was on the floor beside him, and Agnes was still ringing the dinner bell outside the door.

"All right, I heard," he shouted. "Just coming."

He glanced hurriedly over the remains of the packet to see if it bore any mention of the fact that the cut-out garden had magic properties. It did not. He did, however, learn that this was Section Three of the Beautiful Brekkfast Brikk Garden Series, and that Sections One, Two, Four, Five, and Six would be found on other packets. In case of difficulty in obtaining supplies, please write to Fruhstucksgeschirrziegelsteinindustrie (Great Britain), Lily Road, Shepherds Bush.

"Elevenpence a packet," Mark murmured to himself, going to lunch with unwashed hands. "Five elevens are thirty-five. Thirty-five pennies are—no, that's wrong. Fifty-five pence are four-and-sevenpence. Father, if I mow the lawn and carry coal every day for a month, can I have four shillings and sevenpence?"

"You don't want to buy another space gun, do you?" said Mr. Armitage looking at him suspiciously. "Because one is quite enough in this family."

"No, it's not for a space gun, I swear."

"Oh, very well."

"And can I have the four-and-seven now?"

Mr. Armitage gave it reluctantly. "But that lawn has to be like velvet, mind," he said. "And if there's any falling off in the coal supply, I shall demand my money back."

"No, no, there won't be," Mark promised in reply. As soon as lunch was over, he dashed down to Miss Pride's. Was there a chance that she would have sections One, Two, Four, Five, and Six? He felt certain that no other shop had even heard of Brekkfast Brikks, so she was his only hope, apart from the address in Shepherds Bush.

"Oh, I don't know, I'm sure," Miss Pride said, sounding very doubtful—and more than a little surprised. "There might just be a couple on the bottom shelf—yes, here we are."

They were sections Four and Five, bent and dusty, but intact, Mark saw with relief. "Don't you suppose you have any more anywhere?" he pleaded.

"I'll look in the cellar but I can't promise. I haven't had deliveries of any of these for a long time. Made by some foreign firm they were; people didn't seem very keen on them," Miss Pride said aggrievedly. She opened a door revealing a flight of damp stone stairs. Mark followed her down them like a bloodhound on the trail.

The cellar was a fearful confusion of mildewed, tattered, and toppling cartons, some full, some empty. Mark was nearly knocked cold by a shower of pilchards in tins, which he dislodged on to himself from the top of a heap of boxes. At last Miss Pride, with a cry of triumph, unearthed a little cache of Brekkfast Brikks, three packets which turned out to be the remaining sections, Six, One, and Two.

"There, isn't that a piece of luck now!" she said, looking quite faint with all the excitement. It was indeed rare for Miss Pride to sell as many as five packets of the same thing at one time.

Mark galloped home with his booty and met his father on the porch. Mr. Armitage let out a groan of dismay.

"I'd almost rather you'd bought a space gun," he said. Mark chanted in reply:

"Brekkfast Brikks for supper too
Give peaceful sleep the whole night through."

"I don't want peaceful sleep," Mr. Armitage said. "I intend to spend tonight mouse-watching again. I'm tired of finding footprints in the Stilton."

During the next few days Mark's parents watched anxiously to see, Mr. Armitage said, whether Mark would start to sprout esparto grass instead of hair. For he doggedly ate Brekkfast Brikks for lunch, with soup, or sprinkled over his pudding; for tea, with jam, and for supper lightly fried in dripping, not to mention, of course, the immense helpings he had for breakfast with sugar and milk. Mr. Armitage for his part soon gave out; he said he wouldn't taste another Brekkfast Brikk even if it were wrapped in an inch-thick layer of *pâté de foie gras*. Mark regretted that Harriet, who was a handy and uncritical eater, was still away, convalescing from her measles with an aunt.

In two days the second packet was finished (sundial, paved garden, and espaliers). Mark cut it out, fastened it together, and joined it on to Section Three with trembling hands. Would the spell work for this section, too? He sang the rhyme in rather a quavering voice, but luckily the playroom door was shut and there was no one to hear him. Yes! The gate grew again above him, and when he opened it and ran across the lawn through the yew arch, he found himself in a flagged garden full of flowers like huge blue cabbages.

Mark stood hugging himself with satisfaction, and then began to wander about smelling the flowers, which had a spicy perfume most unlike any flower he could think of. Suddenly he pricked up his ears. Had he caught a sound? There! It was like somebody crying and seemed to come from the other side of the hedge. He ran to the next opening and looked through. Nothing: only gray mist and emptiness. But, unless he had imagined it, just before he got there, he thought his eye had caught the flash of white-and-gold draperies swishing past the gateway.

"Do you think Mark's all right?" Mrs. Armitage said to her husband next day. "He seems to be in such a dream all the time."

"Boy's gone clean off his rocker if you ask me," grumbled Mr. Armitage. "It's all these doormats he's eating. Can't be good to stuff your insides with moldy jute. Still I'm bound to say he's cut the lawn very decently and seems to be remembering the coal. I'd better take a day off from the office and drive you over to the shore for a picnic; sea air will do him good."

Mrs. Armitage suggested to Mark that he should slack off on the Brekkfast Brikks, but he was so horrified that she had to abandon the idea. But, she said, he was to run four times round the garden every morning before breakfast. Mark almost said, "Which garden?" but stopped just in time. He had cut out and completed another large lawn, with a lake and weeping willows, and on the far side of the lake had a tantalizing glimpse of a figure dressed in white and gold who moved away and was lost before he could get there.

After munching his way through the fourth packet, he was able to add on a broad grass walk bordered by curiously clipped trees. At the end of the walk he could see the white-and-gold person, but when he ran to the spot, no one was there—the walk ended in the usual gray mist.

When he had finished and had cut out the fifth packet (an orchard), a terrible thing happened to him. For two days he could not remember the tune that worked the spell. He tried other tunes, but they were no use. He sat in the playroom singing till he was hoarse or silent with despair. Suppose he never remembered it again?

His mother shook her head at him that evening and said he looked as if he needed a dose. "It's lucky we're going to Shinglemud Bay for the day tomorrow," she said. "That ought to do you good."

"Oh, *blow*. I'd forgotten about that," Mark said. "Need I go?"

His mother stared at him in utter astonishment.

But in the middle of the night he remembered the right tune, leaped out of bed in a tremendous hurry, and ran down to the playroom without even waiting to put on his dressing gown and slippers.

The orchard was most wonderful, for instead of mere apples its trees bore oranges, lemons, limes and all sorts of tropical fruits whose names he did not know, and there were melons and pineapples growing, and plantains and avocados. Better still, he saw the lady in her white and gold waiting at the end of an alley and was able to draw near enough to speak to her.

"Who are you?" she asked. She seemed very much astonished at the sight of him.

"My name's Mark Armitage," he said politely. "Is this your garden?"

Close to, he saw that she was really very grand indeed. Her dress was white satin embroidered with pearls, and swept the

ground; she had a gold scarf and her hair, dressed high and powdered, was confined in a small gold-and-pearl tiara. Her face was rather plain, pink with a long nose, but she had a kind expression and beautiful gray eyes.

"Indeed it is," she announced with hauteur. "I am Princess Sophia Maria Louisa of Saxe-Hoffenpoffen-und-Hamster. What are you doing here, pray?"

"Well," Mark explained cautiously, "it seemed to come about through singing a tune."

"Indeed. That is most interesting. Did the tune, perhaps, go like this?"

The princess hummed a few bars.

"That's it! How did you know?"

"Why, you foolish boy, it was I who put the spell on the garden, to make it come alive when the tune is played or sung."

"I say!" Mark was full of admiration. "Can you do spells as well as being a princess?"

She drew herself up. "Naturally! At the court of Saxe-Hoffenpoffen, where I was educated, all princesses were taught a little magic, not so much as to be vulgar, just enough to get out of social difficulties."

"Jolly useful," Mark said. "How did you work the spell for the garden, then?"

"Why, you see," (the princess was obviously delighted to have somebody to talk to; she sat on a stone seat and patted it, inviting Mark to do likewise) "I had the misfortune to fall in love with Herr Rudolf, the Court Kapellmeister, who taught me music. Oh, he was so kind and handsome! And he was most talented, but my father, of course, would not hear of my marrying him because he was only a common person."

"So what did you do?"

"I arranged to vanish, of course. Rudi had given me a beautiful book with many pictures of gardens. My father kept strict watch to see I did not run away, so I used to slip between the pages of the book when I wanted to be alone. Then, when we decided to marry, I asked my maid to take the book to Rudi. And I sent him a note telling him to play the tune when he received the book. But I believe that spiteful Gertrud must have played me false and never taken the book, for more than fifty years have now passed and I have been here all alone, waiting in the garden, and Rudi has never come. Oh, Rudi, Rudi," she exclaimed, wringing her hands and crying a little, "where can you be? It is so long—so long!"

"Fifty years," Mark said kindly, reckoning that must make her nearly seventy. "I must say you don't look it."

"Of course I do not, dumbhead. For me, I make it that time does not touch me. But tell me, how did you know the tune that works the spell? It was taught me by my dear Rudi."

"I'm not sure where I picked it up," Mark confessed. "For all I know it may be one of the Top Ten. I'll ask my music teacher, he's sure to know. Perhaps he'll have heard of your Rudolf too."

Privately Mark feared that Rudolf might very well have died by now, but he did not like to depress Princess Sophia Maria by such a suggestion, so he bade her a polite good night, promising to come back as soon as he could with another section of the garden and any news he could pick up.

He planned to go and see Mr. Johansen, his music teacher, next morning, but he had forgotten the family trip to the beach. There was just time to scribble a hasty post card to the British office of Fruhstucksgeschirrziegelsteinindustrie, asking them if they could inform him from what source they had obtained the pictures used on the packets of Brekkfast Brikks.

Then Mr. Armitage drove his wife and son to Shinglemud Bay, gloomily prophesying wet weather.

In fact, the weather turned out fine, and Mark found it quite restful to swim and play beach cricket and eat ham sandwiches and lie in the sun. For he had been struck by a horrid thought: suppose he should forget the tune again when he was inside the garden—would he be stuck there, like Father in the larder? It was a lovely place to go and wander at will, but somehow he didn't fancy spending the next fifty years there with Princess Sophia Maria. Would she oblige him by singing the spell if he forgot it, or would she be too keen on company to let him go? He was not inclined to take any chances.

It was late when they arrived home, too late, Mark thought, to disturb Mr. Johansen, who was elderly and kept early hours. Mark ate a huge helping of sardines on Brekkfast Brikks for supper—he was dying to finish Section Six—but did not visit the garden that night.

Next morning's breakfast (Brikks with hot milk, for a change) finished the last packet—and just as well, for the larder mouse, which Mr. Armitage still had not caught, was discovered to have nibbled the bottom left-hand corner of the packet, slightly damaging an ornamental grotto in a grove of lime trees. Rather worried about this, Mark decided to make up the last section straightaway, in case the magic had been affected. By now he was becoming very skillful at the tiny fiddling task of cutting out the little tabs and slipping them into the little slots; the job did not take long to finish. Mark attached Section Six to Section Five and then, drawing a deep breath, sang the incantation once more. With immense relief he watched the mossy wall and rusty gate grow out of the playroom floor; all was well.

He raced across the lawn, round the lake, along the avenue, through the orchard, and into the lime grove. The scent of the lime flowers was sweeter than a cake baking.

Princess Sophia Maria came towards him from the grotto, looking slightly put out.

"Good morning!" she greeted Mark. "Do you bring me any news?"

"I haven't been to see my music teacher yet," Mark confessed. "I was a bit anxious because there was a hole—"

"Ach, yes, a hole in the grotto! I have just been looking. Some wild beast must have made its way in, and I am afraid it may come again. See, it has made tracks like those of a big bear." She showed him some enormous footprints in the soft sand of the grotto floor. Mark stopped up the hole with prickly branches and promised to bring a dog when he next came, though he felt fairly sure the mouse would not return.

"I can borrow a dog from my teacher—he has plenty. I'll be back in an hour or so—see you then," he said.

"*Auf Wiedersehen*, my dear young friend."

Mark ran along the village street to Mr. Johansen's house, Houndshaven Cottage. He knew better than to knock at the door because Mr. Johansen would be either practicing his violin or out in the barn at the back, and in any case the sound of barking was generally loud enough to drown any noise short of gunfire.

Besides giving music lessons at Mark's school, Mr. Johansen kept a guest house for dogs whose owners were abroad or on holiday. He was extremely kind to the guests and did his best to make them feel at home in every way, finding out from their owners what were their favorite foods, and letting them sleep on his own bed, turn about. He spent all his spare time with them, talking to them and playing either his violin or

long-playing records of domestic sounds likely to appeal to
the canine fancy—such as knives being sharpened, cars starting up, and children playing ball games.

Mark could hear Mr. Johansen playing Brahms' lullaby in
the barn, so he went out there; the music was making some of
the more susceptible inmates feel homesick: howls, sym-
pathetic moans, and long shuddering sighs came from the
numerous comfortably carpeted cubicles all the way down
the barn.

Mr. Johansen reached the end of the piece as Mark entered.
He put down his fiddle and smiled welcomingly.

"Ach, how *gut!* It is the young Mark."

"Hullo, sir."

"You know," confided Mr. Johansen, "I play to many
audiences in my life all over the world, but never anywhere
do I get such a response as from zese dear doggies—it is
really remarkable. But come in, come into ze house and
have some coffee cake."

Mr. Johansen was a gentle, white-haired elderly man; he
walked slowly with a slight stoop and had a kindly, sad
face with large dark eyes. He looked rather like some sort of
dog himself, Mark always thought, perhaps a collie or a long-
haired dachshund.

"Sir," Mark said, "if I whistle a tune to you, can you write
it down for me?"

"Why, yes, I shall be most happy," Mr. Johansen said,
pouring coffee for both of them.

So Mark whistled his tune once more; as he came to the
end, he was surprised to see the music master's eyes fill with
tears, which slowly began to trickle down his thin cheeks.

"It recalls my youth, zat piece," he explained, wiping the
tears away and rapidly scribbling crotchets and minims on a

piece of music paper. "Many times I am whistling it myself—
it is wissout doubt from me you learn it—but always it is re-
minding me of how happy I was long ago when I wrote it."

"You *wrote* that tune?" Mark said, much excited.

"Why yes. What is so strange in zat? Many, many tunes
haf I written."

"Well—" Mark said, "I won't tell you just yet in case I'm
mistaken—I'll have to see somebody else first. Do you mind
if I dash off right away? Oh, and might I borrow a dog—
preferably a good ratter?"

"In zat case, better have my dear Lotta—alzough she is so
old she is ze best of zem all," Mr. Johansen said proudly.
Lotta was his own dog, an enormous shaggy lumbering
animal with a tail like a palm tree and feet the size of
electric polishers; she was reputed to be of incalculable age;
Mr. Johansen called her his strudel-hound. She knew Mark
well and came along with him quite biddably, though it was
rather like leading a mammoth.

Luckily his mother, refreshed by her day at the sea, was
heavily engaged with Agnes the maid in spring cleaning.
Furniture was being shoved about, and everyone was too busy
to notice Mark and Lotta slip into the playroom.

A letter addressed to Mark lay among the clutter on the
table; he opened and read it while Lotta foraged happily
among the piles of magazines and tennis nets and cricket
bats and rusting electronic equipment, managing to upset
several things and increase the general state of huggermug-
ger in the room.

> Dear Sir, (the letter said—it was from Messrs.
> Digit, Digit, & Rule, a firm of chartered account-
> ants)—We are in receipt of your inquiry as to the

source of pictures on packets of Brekkfast Brikks. We are pleased to inform you that these were reproduced from the illustrations of a little-known 18th-century German work, *Steinbergen's Gartenbuch*. Unfortunately the only known remaining copy of this book was burnt in the disastrous fire which destroyed the factory and premises of Messrs. Fruhstucksgeschirrziegelsteinindustrie two months ago. The firm has now gone into liquidation and we are winding up their effects. Yours faithfully, P.J. Zero, Gen. Sec.

"*Steinbergen's Gartenbuch*," Mark thought. "That must have been the book that Princess Sophia Maria used for the spell—probably the same copy. Oh, well, since it's burned, it's lucky the pictures were reproduced on the Brekkfast Brikks packets. Come on, Lotta, let's go and find a nice princess then. Good girl! Rats! Chase 'em!"

He sang the spell and Lotta, all enthusiasm, followed him into the garden.

They did not have to go far before they saw the princess—she was sitting sunning herself on the rim of the fountain. But what happened then was unexpected. Lotta let out the most extraordinary cry—whine, bark, and howl all in one—and hurled herself towards the princess like a rocket.

"Hey! Look out! Lotta! *Heel!*" Mark shouted in alarm. But Lotta, with her great paws on the princess' shoulders, had about a yard of salmon-pink tongue out, and was washing the princess' face all over with frantic affection.

The princess was just as excited. "Lotta, Lotta! She knows me, it's dear Lotta, it must be! Where did you get her?" she cried to Mark, hugging the enormous dog, whose tail was going round faster than a turbo prop.

"Why, she belongs to my music master, Mr. Johansen, and it's he who made up the tune," Mark said.

The princess turned quite white and had to sit down on the fountain's rim again.

"*Johansen*? Rudolf Johansen? My Rudi! At last! After all these years! Oh, run, run, and fetch him immediately, please! Immediately!"

Mark hesitated a moment.

"Please make haste!" she besought him. "Why do you wait?"

"It's only—well, you won't be surprised if he's quite *old*, will you? Remember he hasn't been in a garden keeping young like you."

"All that will change," the princess said confidently. "He has only to eat the fruit of the garden. Why, look at Lotta— when she was a puppy, for a joke I gave her a fig from this tree, and you can see she is a puppy still, though she must be older than any other dog in the world! Oh, please hurry to bring Rudi here."

"Why don't you come with me to his house?"

"That would not be correct etiquette," she said with dignity. "After all, I *am* royal."

"Okay," said Mark. "I'll fetch him. Hope he doesn't think I'm crackers."

"Give him this." The princess took off a locket on a gold chain. It had a miniature of a romantically handsome young man with dark curling hair. "My Rudi," she explained fondly. Mark could just trace a faint resemblance to Mr. Johansen.

He took the locket and hurried away. At the gate something made him look back: the princess and Lotta were sitting at the edge of the fountain, side by side. The princess had an arm round Lotta's neck; with the other hand she waved to him, just a little.

"Hurry!" she called again.

Mark made his way out of the house, through the spring-cleaning chaos, and flew down the village to Houndshaven Cottage. Mr. Johansen was in the house this time, boiling up a noisome mass of meat and bones for the dogs' dinner. Mark said nothing at all, just handed him the locket. He took one look at it and staggered, putting his hand to his heart; anxiously, Mark led him to a chair.

"Are you all right, sir?"

"Yes, yes! It was only ze shock. Where did you get ziss, my boy?"

So Mark told him.

Surprisingly, Mr. Johansen did not find anything odd about the story; he nodded his head several times as Mark related the various points.

"Yes, yes, her letter, I have it still—" he pulled out a worn little scrap of paper, "but ze *Gartenbuch* it reached me never. Zat wicked Gertrud must haf sold it to some bookseller who sold it to Fruhstucksgeschirrziegelsteinindustrie. And so she has been waiting all ziss time! My poor little Sophie!"

"Are you strong enough to come to her now?" Mark asked.

"*Natürlich!* But first we must give ze dogs zeir dinner; zey must not go hungry."

So they fed the dogs, which was a long job as there were at least sixty and each had a different diet, including some very odd preferences like Swiss roll spread with Marmite and yeast pills wrapped in slices of caramel. Privately, Mark thought the dogs were a bit spoiled, but Mr. Johansen was very careful to see that each visitor had just what it fancied.

"After all, zey are not mine! Must I not take good care of zem?"

At least two hours had gone by before the last willow-pattern plate was licked clean, and they were free to go. Mark made rings round Mr. Johansen all the way up the village; the music master limped quietly along, smiling a little; from time to time he said, "Gently, my friend. We do not run a race. Remember I am an old man."

That was just what Mark did remember. He longed to see Mr. Johansen young and happy once more.

The chaos in the Armitage house had changed its location: the front hall was now clean, tidy, and damp; the rumpus of vacuuming had shifted to the playroom. With a black hollow of apprehension in his middle, Mark ran through the open door and stopped, aghast. All the toys, tools, weapons, boxes, magazines, and bits of machinery had been rammed into the cupboards; the floor where his garden had been laid out was bare. Mrs. Armitage was in the playroom taking down the curtains.

"*Mother!* Where's my Brekkfast Brikks garden?"

"Oh, darling, you didn't want it, did you? It was all dusty, I thought you'd finished with it. I'm afraid I've burned it in the furnace. Really you *must* try not to let this room get into such a clutter, it's perfectly disgraceful. Why, hullo, Mr. Johansen," she added in embarrassment. "I didn't see you, I'm afraid you've called at the worst possible moment. But I'm sure you'll understand how it is at spring-cleaning time."

She rolled up her bundle of curtains, glancing worriedly at

Mr. Johansen; he looked rather odd, she thought. But he gave her his tired, gentle smile, and said,

"Why, yes, Mrs. Armitage, I understand, I understand very well. Come, Mark. We have no business here, you can see."

Speechlessly, Mark followed him. What was there to say?

"Never mind," Mrs. Armitage called after Mark. "The Rice Nuts pack has a helicopter on it."

Every week in *The Times* newspaper you will see this advertisement:

BREKKFAST BRIKKS PACKETS. £100
offered for any in good condition,
whether empty or full.

So, if you have any, you know where to send them.

But Mark is growing anxious; none have come in yet, and every day Mr. Johansen seems a little thinner and more elderly. Besides, what will the princess be thinking?

JOAN AIKEN, daughter of American writer Conrad Aiken, was born in Rye, Sussex, England. She has engaged in a variety of work, including features editor for a magazine and a copywriter for a large London advertising agency. Now she devotes her time to writing.

Her hobbies are painting and gardening at her home, an ex-pub in Petworth, England, where she lives with her two teen-age children.

Artist BETTY FRASER was born and grew up in Boston, Massachusetts. Since graduating from the Rhode Island School of Design she has had a very busy career in the fields of advertising and book illustration. Miss Fraser is now a resident of New York City's Greenwich Village, and claims herself addicted to reading, raising plants and talking!